"You look lost."

Leslie felt a betraying clenching in her chest. Half in incomprehensible fear, half in anticipation, she turned toward the softly drawling voice. Leaning back against the cabinet in an alcove beside the refrigerator was the man who could forever change her life.

The feeling that had started when she left the airport, that had grown stronger each minute since she'd entered David's house—the knowledge that this was not some harmless, romantic fantasy but a reality she wasn't sure she could go through with—held her immobile.

She stood in the middle of the room, unable to do more than silently study the darkly attractive face she'd thought would be familiar to her, the unsmiling shadowed eyes of a stranger.

She swallowed once and prayed her voice would work. "I think I *am* lost."

Slowly the lean figure in snug, faded jeans and an equally faded blue shirt uncoiled from his relaxed pose and crossed the room to stand in front of her. "I didn't think this would be so awkward," he said in his soft drawl.

Leslie felt her own hesitant, answering smile. "Neither did I."

Mary Modean

After years of extensive traveling throughout the midwest securing oil and gas leases, Mary Modean has at last fulfilled two long-standing dreams: becoming a full-time writer and returning to the comfort and familiarity of a permanent home.

She now lives in a restored Victorian farm home overlooking a small town in the mountains of southeastern Oklahoma with a matriarchal dog, a varying number of black cats, and, reportedly, a resident ghost.

She enjoys wandering the nearby hills once traveled by pre-Columbian mound builders, Viking explorers, and transplanted Indians, but more important to her are the people of her adopted home and renewing friendships that, despite her long absences, have survived.

Dear Reader:

We're very excited to be able to offer you author Mary Modean's first book for Second Chance at Love, the deeply moving *In Name Only* (#400). Threatened with losing custody of her son Mike, Leslie Burgess flees the east coast, seeking refuge in rural Oklahoma and a marriage of convenience to rancher and veterinarian David Nichols. Sublimating past sorrows, David and Leslie work hard to pull their lives together. But he's trapped by a secret burden of pain he's afraid to share...and she's unprepared for the soul-stirring depth of desire this lean, quiet man arouses within her. Mary Modean delivers with emotionally complex characters whose compelling—and very real—love story will leave you anxious for more from this talented author.

You won't be disappointed in Liz Grady's fresh take on a "coming to terms with the past" theme in this month's *Reclaim the Dream* (#401). Washington protocol expert Laurel Forrest seems the perfect product of a classy upbringing, moving through the corridors of power with ease and sophistication...until her long-ago love, brawny maverick Sawyer Gates shows up and threatens to shatter her facade. Only Sawyer knows the lie she's built her life on, and Laurel's got to finagle her way out of being exposed. But somehow the heat of Sawyer's gaze sparks a need, and Laurel's not sure she wants to escape the danger of his strong embrace...Liz Grady leads you through a maze of love and deception to a delightfully satisfying conclusion in this, her ninth, Second Chance at Love.

Carolina Moon (#402) by Joan Darling combines exciting romance with hilarious domestic comedy for surefire entertainment. When the man of her dreams moves next door and proceeds to sweep her off her feet, Eileen "Fergie" Duffy can scarcely believe her good fortune. But her ardent neighbor, Ryan O'Donnell, has no use for children—and Fergie, a widow, happens to be the mother of three! Her kids adore Ryan, though; they unanimously decide to adopt him—and every time Ryan looks at Fergie, his resolve crumbles. The house next door starts to feel like home, and Fergie's the one woman who can make him happy...Author Joan Darling confesses she based Ryan on *Moonlighting's* Bruce Willis, and he's certainly a hunk with a sense of humor, not to mention fatal charm.

Diana Morgan exhibits more marvelous madness this month with *The Wedding Belle* (#403). Intrigued by a mysterious blonde decked out in bridal finery while she is stationed in the middle of the Chattahoochee River, patrician venture capitalist Ned Fontaine introduces himself. Soon he's introducing Jolie MacGregor to his family as *his* bride in a nonmarriage of convenience. Ned will stake Jolie as she opens a high-fashion boutique, while she'll keep unmarried Southern belles and their anxious mamas away from Ned. This perfect arrangement takes some interesting turns when Ned and Jolie fall madly in love! With the heady mist of a fine champagne, Diana Morgan presents a characteristically memorable romantic romp.

Laine Allen brings lively romance to a department store setting in *Courting Trouble* (#404), when Personnel Manager Claire Kendrick takes on an ex-convict as an employee. Mace Dawson's good looks are truly criminal—and his answers to the company questionnaire are downright impertinent. Claire's boss insists it will do this con-man good to work under her protective wing—but it's Claire's heart that needs protection when Mace starts to undo all her rules and regulations. Claire doesn't know that Mace is merely masquerading as a man in need of reform; he's actually the head of an outreach program for ex-convicts, and wants to learn how it feels to be a second-class citizen. Claire's already falling fast—and there's plenty of first-class banter as these two *try* to work together...

A widowed mother finds love again in *Everybody's Hero* (#405) by Second Chance star Jan Mathews. Delaney Anderson never wanted her seventeen-year-old son to join the Marines—and she certainly never expected to fall in love with his recruiting officer! Captain Lloyd Thomas is an officer and a gentleman, but Delaney's past with the military is a tragic one. She's afraid her years of heartbreak won't let her give in to Lloyd's sense of fun, yet he soon lures her into a schoolgirl's romance that leaves her breathless. Delaney learns to give up some of her maternal obligations, and Jan portrays her passionate rejuvenation with grace and good-natured humor. *Everybody's Hero* is another winner from an all-time Second Chance favorite, topping off a month of spring surprises.

Happy Reading!

Joan Marlow

Joan Marlow, Editor
SECOND CHANCE AT LOVE
The Berkley Publishing Group
200 Madison Avenue
New York, NY 10016

MARY MODEAN
IN NAME ONLY

**A
SECOND CHANCE AT LOVE
BOOK**

To Paula B., for picking me up and pushing me on, for feeding me when times got tough, and for once again lending me a son, although this time even she won't recognize him. Here's to fireplaces, computers, good music, and the time to enjoy them all.

IN NAME ONLY

Chapter

1

THIS MIGHT BE the most foolish thing she had ever done. Leslie acknowledged the thought—and dismissed it with her next one: Desperate women take desperate steps.

She turned to look at her son, asleep in the back seat of the Buick, but all she could see was the pale blur of Mike's cotton-white hair against the dark upholstery. She spared a glance for Hank Baker, the wiry, weathered man David had sent to meet them, but he was scowling straight ahead, so she resumed her silent vigil of the night-shrouded trees, dark and impenetrable, looming on each side of the narrow road.

She hadn't realized just how desperate this step was until an hour before, when they'd left the airport at Fort

Smith, Arkansas, and headed south and west into the mountains of southeastern Oklahoma.

Leslie had known the ranch was isolated—David had told her that much in his first letter—but she'd had no real concept of what "isolated" meant in rural Oklahoma. It was so *dark*. While she hadn't expected an endless metropolitan area, she'd expected at least to see clusters of lights indicating neighbors within sight of each other; but for the last twenty minutes, she'd seen nothing—not even another car.

She heard the clicking of the turn signal and looked toward Hank as he veered onto a narrow unpaved road and stopped the car. "Miz Burgess," he said in a soft, flat voice. He gripped the steering wheel, not looking at her. "Doc has had his share of grief, more grief than a man ought to have to bear. If you're bringing him more, I can turn around and take you back to the airport."

Leslie sighed and sank back against the seat. David had told her that Hank was loyal, but actually hearing the loyalty in the man's voice was the needed confirmation that David had not lied, about that or about anything else.

She attempted a reassuring smile but realized how futile that was in the darkness of the car. "I have never intentionally hurt anyone, Mr. Baker," she told him, "and I don't intend to start with David Nichols."

Hank grunted, a short, one-syllable sound that could have meant anything, but he eased his foot onto the accelerator. He was only partially satisfied with her answer, she knew, and of course he was curious about her . . . but no more curious than she was about the man she'd come halfway across the country to see.

She'd thought she knew David Nichols, through his letters, the pictures he'd sent, the lengthy telephone conversations. But in these foreign surroundings, she felt her confidence waning. Letters could be edited—hers had been. She had raked her soul in an attempt to be honest with him but had pared and whittled and chiseled down her words until the letters she'd finally mailed only hinted at what she'd gone through. Pictures could lie. Telephone conversations, no matter how lengthy, were not so long that one couldn't play a role. David was a caring, sensitive man. Leslie clutched at that thought, a needed lifeline in the darkness enveloping her.

If only he'd met her at the airport himself, instead of sending Hank . . . but he hadn't. An emergency, Hank had explained. A mare in foal. A caring, sensitive man, Leslie repeated silently. In the hour's drive, she and David could have overcome their initial awkwardness, could even now be discussing the future. Or maybe not, she thought. Maybe they would be sitting in the same heavy silence she now shared with Hank.

Hank made another turn, and Leslie felt the car climbing again. After a few hundred yards, they broke through the trees into a large clearing. She saw two houses and a cluster of barns, all shining with security lights but widely spaced, affording each area the semblance of privacy. The interior of one barn was lighted, as was that of one of the houses, and on first impression Leslie thought the brightly lit barn seemed more welcoming than the low-lying hulk of a house where a muted glow came from only two windows.

Hank drove toward the house, though, down a small slope and onto a graveled area where he parked beside a dark-colored Cadillac, and Leslie could see from the lighted entryway that the house was not as low lying as she'd first thought. It was a split-level, built on the edge of a ridge, its details still hidden in shadows.

Hank stepped from the car and began unloading suitcases from the trunk. Leslie got out, stretched, and opened the back door.

"Mike," she said gently, touching the sleeping boy on the shoulder. Once she would have carried him, letting him stay lost in sleep, but now he was almost as tall as she was. "Wake up, honey. We're here."

Mike sat up slowly, still groggy and disoriented, and stared at her mutely.

"We're here," she repeated softly. "Come on, get out of the car."

She helped him stumble from the car. Then, slinging the strap of the tote bag over her shoulder and picking up one of the cases, she guided him through the door into the house—following Hank, who carried their other three bags—and up a short flight of stairs.

Another short flight had led down, and Leslie realized that, had the lights been on in the lower level, the downstairs would have been visible over the half-wall of the hallway. Another half-wall separated the rooms on the upper floor from the hall, but everything was open and spacious. The two lighted windows she had seen from the outside were a breakfast room and the kitchen, but they hurried past them and up still another shorter flight of stairs to the bedroom wing.

David *had* lied to her, Leslie thought, but his lies had been lies of omission. His house was new, he'd told her, barely four years old, built near his parents' original ranch home where Hank, his foreman, and Mabel, Hank's wife, now lived; but he hadn't told her it was strikingly modern, almost daring in concept. And he hadn't told her that he had the kind of wealth necessary to build and maintain such a home. That bothered her. That "little" omission also went a long way toward explaining Hank's barely concealed suspicions of her.

Hank nodded to his right as they passed a closed door. "Mrs. Nichols's room," he said. "She got here this afternoon." He nodded to his left. "And Ellie's."

The room alloted to Mike, next to Ellie's, was definitely a boy's room. Tommy's, Leslie thought. The son who would have been Mike's age.

"I'll put your stuff in the room right across the hall,"

Hank told her, looking questioningly at the bags. Smiling hesitantly, Leslie showed him which were hers and began a polite thank you. "Just part of the job," he muttered. "I'd better go out to the barn and see if Doc needs any help."

Leslie supervised as Mike tugged out of his clothes and finished in the adjoining bathroom, then she tucked him into bed, but the mechanics of her actions couldn't distract her from the coolness of her reception. When she stepped from Mike's bedroom, Hank had gone.

Leslie stepped into the softly lighted room across the hall. Her bags had been placed at the foot of the bed.

Now what was she supposed to do? Leslie wondered as she stood alone in the pleasant, spacious room. How was it possible to feel so alone in a house full of sleeping people? *Stop it!* Leslie told herself. It was simply the lateness of the hour, and her own imagination, making her feel like an unwelcome intruder.

Leaving her suitcases untouched, Leslie walked into the adjoining bathroom. She had freshened her makeup before the plane landed, but the glaring lights of this well-appointed bath mocked her earlier efforts. She was tired, and it showed in the shadows beneath her eyes— and in her eyes themselves, now a dull, lusterless brown. What was expected of her? Should she, too, go to bed, or should she go to the barn and seek out David? She shook her head defiantly. There was no way she would just sink into the oblivion of sleep without having first seen him. For a moment she considered changing clothes, then decided not to. She had chosen to wear the yellow dress because it traveled well, and it had.

Realizing her indecision for what it was—an avoidance of the impending meeting—she ran a brush through her shoulder-length hair the color of dark honey. She grimaced. Tonight even her hair looked as lifeless and exhausted as she felt. None of its highlights glowed—not the gold, not the red. She applied light blusher and a fresh coat of peach lip gloss and studied her reflection critically. Surely that would be sufficient. After all, it was after midnight, and she had traveled across half a continent.

She looked in on Mike, recognizing the action for the loving procrastination it was, and found him sleeping peacefully. "I hope I'm doing the right thing, baby," she whispered.

Ellie's door stood slightly ajar, and from within came the soft glow of a night light. Leslie paused in the hall. She would meet the girl at breakfast, but curiosity and something stronger made her reach out to the door, push it open, and slip into the room. She stood silently, letting her eyes adjust to the dimness and trying to understand what she had committed herself to do.

"Daddy?"

The girl's voice startled her. Fuller than she remembered from the telephone conversations, it was still a small sound in the darkness. "No, Ellie," she said softly, hoping that finding a stranger in her bedroom wouldn't frighten the child too much. "It's Leslie. I'm sorry I woke you."

"Oh." Ellie turned on her side, facing her. "Daddy said you might come."

Leslie smiled at the girl. Daddy had said she *might* come. So David hadn't been as sure she would actually get on the plane as he'd sounded.

All color had been leeched to shades of gray in the half-light of the room, but Leslie could make out Ellie's features. A long braid hung over each shoulder—dark brown, Leslie knew from the snapshots—and large, expressive eyes dominated a thin face that was much too wise and much too old for Ellie's nine years.

"Is Mike with you?" Ellie asked in a sleep-thickened voice.

"Yes. He's asleep in the next room."

"Mmm." Ellie covered a yawn with her hand. "Where's Daddy?"

Leslie took a step closer, encouraged by the girl's lack of alarm, and then another step. Almost without realizing it, she was at the bedside, smoothing the tangled sheet. "Hank said he was still at the barn."

"Still?" A little pout of disappointment quickly widened into another sleepy yawn. "He always says good night to me. You won't let him forget, will you?"

"No," Leslie told her gently. "I won't let him forget." Fighting an urge to brush the stray tendrils of hair from Ellie's forehead, she turned to leave the room

"Leslie." Ellie's voice stopped her at the door. She turned to face the bed. "I'm glad you came."

Leslie felt the sting of moisture in her eyes at the first real words of welcome she'd heard. She had to force her reply past the tightness in her throat. "Thank you."

The lower part of the house remained in darkness, compounding her growing sense of isolation. Still not sure what she should do, Leslie walked into the dimly lighted kitchen.

"You look lost."

Leslie felt a betraying clenching in her chest. Half in incomprehensible fear, half in anticipation, she turned toward the softly drawling voice. Leaning back against the cabinet in an alcove beside the refrigerator was the man who could forever change her life.

The feeling that had started when she left the airport, that had grown stronger each minute since she'd entered David's house—the knowledge that this was not some harmless, romantic fantasy but a reality she wasn't sure she could go through with—held her immobile.

She stood in the middle of the room, unable to do more than silently study the darkly attractive face she'd thought would be familiar to her, the unsmiling shadowed eyes of a stranger.

She swallowed once and prayed her voice would work. "I think I *am* lost."

Slowly the lean figure in snug, faded jeans and an equally faded blue shirt uncoiled from his relaxed pose and crossed the room to stand in front of her. Still motionless, Leslie continued to look up at his face. Now that David was no longer in shadow, she could see the unspoken question in his dark brown eyes and the first sign of warmth, the beginning of a wry smile that softened the harsh planes of his face.

"I didn't think this would be so awkward," he said in his soft drawl.

Leslie felt her own hesitant, answering smile. "Neither did I."

"My mother went on to bed, partly because it's so late, but mostly, I suspect, to give us some privacy for this meeting."

Leslie nodded. Privacy? Privacy for what? Now that she actually faced him, all the questions that had seemed so important fled from her mind. "Is the mare all right?"

"Yes." His smile deepened, warming his eyes, and completely transforming him from someone who, only a moment before, had seemed cold and harsh, into the man of Leslie's imagination. "Yes. She's fine. She was cleaning the foal when I left." His smile faded, and he looked at her questioningly. "I have to go back in a few minutes to make sure the foal gets on her feet and starts nursing, but Hank told me you were here. I wanted to see you—to welcome you—before it got any later. I'm sorry I couldn't be at the airport to meet you."

Leslie felt a suspicious tightening in her throat. She was sorry he hadn't been there, too, but it seemed somehow petty to mention it now. "That's all right," she said. "I understand."

Her words were a polite fiction. She didn't understand, not really, any more than she understood why this meeting was so difficult. And as they stood there silently, David apparently no more able to make conversation than she was, Leslie grew even more uncomfortable. She should have changed, she thought frantically as she felt him studying her. Her bravado of a few minutes before had deserted her as quickly as her words had; she felt travel-stained and weary and sensed, irrationally or not, that he found her less than he expected. His continued silence only intensified that fear.

"Would you like to see them?" he asked.

Lost in her thoughts, it took Leslie a moment to realize that David was talking about the mare and new foal. She glanced up at him, and her surprise must have shown in her face. Whatever she'd imagined they might say to each other, whatever she'd imagined they would do, her fantasies of their first meeting had never included traipsing to a barn in the middle of the night to visit a horse. But this was her new life, she reminded herself, a life she sought out for herself and for Mike, and one to which she would adjust. She felt a smile playing with her lips as she considered just how much she had to learn. "Yes," she said. "I'd like that very much."

David seemed to relax a little with her words. "Good," he told her. "We don't have to stay long."

He led her out through the French doors in the breakfast room. Moonlight danced over the surrounding mountains, gently lighting the areas between the security lights. Leslie felt dry grass beneath her sandals, a breeze gently lifting her hair, and heard the strange night sounds—no car engines, horns, or sirens, but a threateningly unfamiliar and unidentifiable mixture of insect, bird, and animal noises. She glanced at the man walking confidently beside her and took comfort in his presence; surely nothing here could be any more dangerous than a late night trip to the grocery store in her old neighborhood.

Most of the lights had been turned off in the barn. "Watch your step here," David told her as they reached the doorway, but he made no move to touch her. She smiled her gratitude at the warning and stepped into the darkened building where only one light glowed at the opposite end of a long hallway. Here, too, the sensations were alien to her—the scent of hay, the unfamiliar structure, neatly stored tools only partially visible in the dim light, and David beside her seeming so much a part of his surroundings.

The mare was in a stall near the light. David stopped in front of the stall, turning toward Leslie and gesturing toward the mare and foal. "Her timing could have been better," he said, and Leslie sensed he was still trying to explain why he'd sent someone else for her instead of coming himself.

"Or mine," Leslie said.

He shook his head. "Of the two arrivals today, yours is far more important, Leslie." He stepped back. "Would you like to take a closer look?"

She'd needed his words, his reassurance. Smiling, she stepped up to the rails surrounding the stall and peered through. The closest she'd ever been to a horse was on a carousel, but the beauty of the mare was apparent even to her. And the foal—ungainly, barely on its feet, and nuzzling hungrily at its mother—showed promise of being every bit as beautiful.

Leslie glanced at David. He was studying the foal as intently as he'd studied her in the kitchen, but his face showed his pride in the animals, in the delivery he'd assisted. His hands rested on the rail in front of him, and Leslie noticed them for the first time. Competent hands. Caring hands. Long-fingered, with neat, square-cut nails. They were roughened from hard work, but they were a healer's hands.

For the first time since he'd spoken to her in the kitchen, he seemed completely at ease. And he should be. They were in his world. Her world now, she promised. She would make it her world. It wouldn't be simple—she thought of all the steps that had led her to this point—nothing in her life had been simple for so long that Leslie doubted she'd recognize something if it were. But with Mike beginning to run fiercely with the wrong crowd, with the end of her job in an economically depressed city, and with Mike's grandparents, who had ignored him for most of his life except to sporadically shower him lavishly with expensive gifts—suddenly threatening to take Mike as a replacement for the son they'd so easily abandoned when he married Leslie —she had known that simple steps, accepted steps, *usual* steps, wouldn't be enough. She'd had to get Mike out of Paterson, away from his friends and away from the steadily growing threat of losing him forever.

When Madge, her neighbor, had first shown her a personal column, Leslie hadn't considered it as anything she'd ever want to use. Writing an ad and deciding to place it had been one of the most difficult things she'd ever done. But she hadn't used any of the urban papers. Starting with *The Western Horseman* and *Progressive Farmer,* she'd located six magazines that were targeted to the kind of man who could provide Mike with the home she wanted him to have—and who could provide her with the anonymity and security of a place Leta and Harrison Burgess would never think to look for her.

"Urban widow," her ad had read, "28, petite, brown eyes, light brown hair, seeks farmer/rancher to 40 as husband and as father for her twelve-year-old son." Not all of the magazines had carried personal columns, but all had classified ads, and most of them had accepted hers. There hadn't been many replies. Only one had gotten past the second letter to the telephone call stage, and that had been from David Nichols. Thirty-five, a widower, someone who had, himself, lost a son, he seemed able to understand what she was going through.

They had spoken of love, but it played no part in their bargain. Well, she thought as she pushed herself away from the rail and looked up at him, that was fine with her. She knew from her experience with Michael Burgess how quickly romantic love faded, and what kinds of problems it could cause. The only worthwhile thing that had come from her encounter with it was Mike. She had paid dearly for her determination to bear her son and to raise him, and if the only way she could keep him was to marry a man she didn't love, to forgo forever the possibility of an elusive dream, then it was a small price compared with all that had gone before.

But looking at David now in the dim light, she wondered for the first time if she would come to regret their bargain. What if someday, instead of counting all the good things this marriage could bring, she would begin to resent the loss of something she had once considered negligible?

She and David would be friends, Leslie repeated to herself as she had so many times before. They would be companions, they would even be—she hesitated at the thought, then hurried through it as she always had, although, with him standing so close, so disturbingly *real*, in the shadowed intimacy of the barn, she had to force herself to go on—they would even be lovers, and between them they would raise two fine children. That would be enough, she vowed. *That would be enough.*

David glanced over at her. With an uncanny perception, he seemed to sense where her thoughts had strayed. "Was it difficult for you? Getting away?"

"No," she admitted. In fact, after all of her worrying, it had been ridiculously easy, but she hadn't been relaxed until she and Mike had boarded the plane at Newark International. "But it's been an awfully long day."

"For me, too." He paused in uneasy silence. "Are you hungry?"

She shook her head.

"Then why don't you go on to bed now? We can talk in the morning." He turned and walked with her toward the house. "My lawyer will be out tomorrow afternoon with the agreement, and I thought we could go into town the next day and take care of the formalities."

"So soon?" she asked, unable to hide her new uncertainty.

"Leslie, is there anything you haven't told me?"

She took a deep breath. Was there? Had she been absolutely honest with him? "Lots of things," she said finally, knowing that this, too, was honest. "Just as I am sure there are lots of things you haven't told me. But nothing that will change the truth of what I've said. Nothing that will make any difference."

"Then why postpone it? It's why you're here; it's why I asked you here. Waiting, even a few days, can't do anything but give you more time to worry. Or to change your mind. Have you changed your mind?"

"No. Of course not."

"I don't think they can do it," David said gently. "I don't think any court in the land would take Mike away from you and give him to grandparents who have stood by and watched you struggling to raise him without giving you any more help than you say they have. Not even with the problems he's been having lately."

"Maybe not," she admitted. "But I can't run that risk. The Burgesses have money, and influence, and they know there's no way on earth that I can afford to fight them on their own terms."

"In the morning," he promised, "this won't seem quite so ominous to you." He smiled gently at her small start of surprise but said nothing about it. "In the morning, I'll meet Mike, and you'll meet Ellie—"

"I met her tonight," Leslie told him, interrupting his assurances even though she needed to hear them. "She asked me to remind you to say good night. She's—she's a beautiful child."

"Yes. Yes, she is."

Stopping at the doors to the breakfast room, he lifted his hand to Leslie's cheek, and she marveled at the sensations that spread through her at his tentative touch—comfort, yes, as she'd come to expect from him, but also something much stronger, something she couldn't yet let herself explore.

"And you're a beautiful woman. You could have found someone closer to home."

Could she have? Would that be a question that rose to haunt her after she'd taken the irrevocable step? "Maybe," she said hesitantly, "if I'd had the opportunity to look. And you, David, you could have found someone closer to home, too."

"Maybe," he admitted quietly. "If I'd wanted to look."

She knew too well what he meant. He had been almost brutally honest in his letters. She knew that the memory of his wife Elaine was still precious to him, even though it had been two years since her small plane had crashed, killing her and their ten-year-old son and injuring Ellie. Leslie knew that David wanted to be married, wanted the stability of a home, wanted a mother for Ellie, even wanted her son, but with Leslie he didn't have to pretend a love he didn't, and might never, feel.

Standing there, however, surrounded by the night noises and soft breeze, with his slightly calloused hand still cupping her cheek, his eyes hidden in shadows, all of those things faded from importance. They were just a man and woman, in the dark, headed for intimacy. The tension intensified between them, drawing them closer together. Would he kiss her? Was this where the moment was leading? But as her unspoken thoughts hung heavily around her she realized that he'd made no move to bring her physically closer, and that she *couldn't* make that move.

Leslie sighed and turned her face, breaking the contact. "Good night, then," she said in the soft, hushed voice that seemed appropriate for the night.

Chapter

2

"DADDY, SHE'S BEAUTIFUL!" Ellie's voice echoed through the barn, dim and cool even in the threatened heat of the July morning.

David grinned unashamedly as he lifted his daughter onto the wooden rail surrounding the stall which housed Kafka the mare and her new foal. This was how he wanted to see Ellie, enthusiastic, alive. For a while, at least, she had shed the veneer of seeming not to care too much about anything or anyone. For a while, she had been the child he'd been searching for behind the dark, shadowed eyes and quiet, undemanding manner.

The quarter horses had been Elaine's—a passion which had gripped her since long before he'd met her when they were both pre-vet students at Oklahoma State—all hers except for Kafka, who somehow had unofficially become Ellie's when the mare was no older than the ungainly filly now nudging her flank. An injury when she was a two-year-old had ended Kafka's racing career, but Elaine had been no more able to get rid of her then than David had been able to later, when he sold the rest of the stable of racing stock.

The mare's real value, he knew, was in the pleasure she brought his daughter, the sparkle in Ellie's eyes, the laughter in her voice, the excitement which filled her small body.

He made sure that Ellie was secure on her perch and turned to the boy standing beside him. "Mike?"

"Yes, sir?"

"Do you want to climb up so that you can get a better look?"

David turned away from the boy so that Mike wouldn't misinterpret his smile, hooked his boot over the first rail, and lifted himself onto the fence, casually showing Mike how it was done and that it really was all right to do so. Mike had his own veneer, an overlay of streetwise toughness, a world-weary *you-can't-surprise-me-I've-seen-it-all* attitude that made him, in a way, just as vulnerable as Ellie. But underneath all that, David could see that Mike was basically a good boy, well mannered, well trained in the basics of living. Leslie had done a good job with him. She had a right to be proud—and protective.

David felt the boy move onto the fence. Still casual, he rested his elbows on the top rail and waited. After a moment's pause, Mike raised himself up another rail and rested his elbows on the top in nonchalant imitation.

"Isn't she beautiful, Mike?" Ellie asked in a hushed voice. "She's going to be just like her mother when she grows up."

"Sure."

David glanced at the boy. Kafka was watching the

three of them warily, but no more warily than Mike was eyeing the horse.

"She's nervous," David told him. "She knows Ellie and I won't hurt her. She doesn't know about you yet, but unless you threaten her foal, she won't attack."

Kafka sidled closer to the fence, moving her head toward Mike's hand. Mike didn't move away, but David saw the color blanch from the boy's face as he struggled to hold onto his relaxed pose.

"She wants a treat," Ellie said, "but she'll settle for a scratch on the nose."

When Mike didn't move, Ellie reached across her father, feathering her hand up the long slope of the mare's head. "Like this."

Slowly Mike reached out. David didn't know if it was the attraction of the horse or the challenge of a girl naturally doing something that was so alien to him, but in a moment Mike was running his fingers across Kafka as if he'd been doing it all his life. When Kafka whuffed gently, Mike looked up at David, for a moment forgetting to hide his feelings. "I think she likes me."

"I think you're right." David gave Kafka a scratch behind her ear before hopping from the fence and lifting Ellie down. "But I also think we've stayed long enough."

David fought back a wave of frustration as the excitement left Ellie's eyes and she shrank back into her shell of politeness. "Would you like me to show Mike around?" she asked in what he recognized as an unconscious mimicry of the way Elaine had once freed him from acting as tour guide for visiting buyers or business associates.

But in this case, Ellie's suggestion made sense. Leslie was alone in the house. He'd insisted that no one disturb her this morning while she got what was obviously much needed rest, but he didn't want her awakening disoriented and as apprehensive as she'd been the night before with nothing but her thoughts to keep her company. And it would be good for the children; they had to get to know each other. Who could tell? Perhaps in the wilds of the unknown, Mike would let some of who he really was slip out. Perhaps in showing someone new the ranch and animals she loved, Ellie would let something of her real self surface.

"I think that would be a good idea," David told her, then leaned back against the rails of the stall as he watched the two children walk outside into the sunlight.

He and Leslie were doing the right thing, but why, now, did he find it necessary to keep reminding himself of that? He knew himself well enough to realize that his doubts were not caused by any sense of betraying Elaine or the marriage they'd shared. He had deeply loved Elaine—still did, he admitted, even though he knew he needed to let go of that love, let it assume its proper place in his life and his memories. Beautiful, dark haired and dark eyed, full of the joy of living, even after eleven years of marriage, she had challenged him daily. Their son Tommy had been a unique combination of the best qualities of both of them and a constant source of wonder to David. Losing them had left him not with an emptiness but with a huge wound which he wasn't sure would ever heal.

But he was also aware of Ellie's needs. He didn't know how to raise a daughter, especially a daughter whose memories and sense of loss were as vivid as his own. Ellie needed the constant, gentling influence of a mother figure, and David hadn't been sure he would ever be able to provide her with that.

David had seen Leslie's ad accidentally, but he'd been drawn back to it time after time. She had asked for a father for her twelve-year-old son; Tommy would have been twelve. Finally, almost against his will, David answered the ad. To his surprise, he found Leslie to be soft-spoken and attractive, with a gentle sense of humor.

She explained her situation and her reasons for advertising in a straightforward manner. And as her situation worsened she'd met it with varying degrees of stoicism or optimism but never with any sign of hysteria.

During the weeks that they wrote and talked with each other on the telephone, David came to accept that Leslie would be a calming influence for Ellie and for him—soothing, without the fire and flash Elaine had possessed. She wouldn't ask more of him than he could give, nor would she attempt to give him more than he could accept. He would help spare her the threatened loss of her son, she would help him raise his daughter, and together they would be . . . content. Contentment was more than most people had; it was certainly more than he'd thought he would ever find again.

What he hadn't expected was the need to protect her that had swept over him when he first saw her, alone and lost, in his kitchen the night before. What he hadn't expected was the equally swift jolt of desire he'd felt when he no more than touched her face.

It was a natural reaction, he supposed, trying to put those emotions into perspective. He had been alone for a long time. He'd be lying to himself if he denied that he had thought of her sexually. He wasn't altruistic enough even to try to convince himself that he and Leslie could have come this far—in what his mother blatantly called a plan conceived by idiots—had she not been someone he could desire.

He liked Leslie, he reminded himself as he started toward the house. He felt that he knew her. He respected her. He admired the way she had faced her problems and had set out to find a way to keep Mike with her in spite of what at times must have seemed insurmountable odds. And they *were* doing the right thing.

* * *

David was waiting for her, alone, in the sun-washed breakfast room. He stood as Leslie entered the room, and she paused just inside the doorway.

One thing she had to remember, she told herself as she looked across the room at him, was that he must be feeling as awkward and unsure of his actions as she was. A first date was bad enough, but here it was, the day before the wedding, and the pressure was unbearable.

But those facts still didn't give her a clue about how to act toward him, she realized as she watched a questioning shadow momentarily darken his eyes. She could no more be gushingly affectionate than she could be coldly matter-of-fact. And she didn't believe he wanted her to act either of those ways—or to "act" at all.

Friends, she reminded herself as she walked toward him; new friends, it was true, but friends who had promised to share a future.

"Good morning," she said, smiling hesitantly.

"Good morning," he answered in the soft drawl she'd admired since their first conversation. His accent wasn't southern, he'd told her, far from it, but to her ears it sounded southern, soft, caressing, a voice of someone who would never be in too much of a hurry to really talk with someone else.

"I'm sorry I slept so late."

"You were tired." He dismissed her apology with a tentative smile of his own. "I could tell that last night. Don't worry about it." He indicated a chair and Leslie hesitantly sat down. "I had things to take care of until just a while ago, anyway. Coffee?" he asked.

Leslie nodded.

"Cream? Sugar?" A chuckle broke from him, and as

Leslie recognized the irony in their situation, her soft laughter joined his.

"We have a lot to learn about each other, don't we?"

"Yes," she said, "we do. I take my coffee black, and I'm incapable of fitting words into sentences until I've had at least two cups." She felt her smile slipping. In the beginning, when he'd had no more reality for her than words on pages, she'd found no trouble baring her thoughts. She couldn't let herself abandon that honesty now. "And I'm feeling really strange, sitting here, having this conversation with you."

David paused in his reach for the coffee pot. "I know," he admitted, "and nothing but spending some time together is going to get us through this initial uneasiness. We meet with Phil at three this afternoon, and sometime today we need to talk with the children, but other than that, the day is ours."

David walked to her side and dropped one hand lightly on her shoulder. "Would you like me to show you around your home?"

Leslie looked up at him, trying to hide the tension his touch brought. "Yes," she said softly, "I would."

Leslie relaxed against the trunk of an ancient oak tree as the sunlight dappling through the leaves played across her face.

Below the house, the land fell away sharply to a small, cleared valley. The sun was high in the pale, almost colorless July sky, hanging in a shimmering haze over forested mountains that stretched as far as she could see. Cleared pastures were visible here and there, but the rest of the landscape was covered with trees— pine and oak, if those close to the house were any indication, but unidentifiable in the distance as they colored the gentle mountains in shades of green, darkening to violet, darkening to blue.

To the south of the house, the land had been cleared for barns, working pastures, and even a hangar and small grass landing strip. To the north, however, the woodlands were virtually untouched, and it was in that direction David had guided her after lunch.

She glanced at him now, seated beside her on the bank of a small creek barely active in the middle of July but still providing a cool, restful scene. He rested his elbows on his knees as he idly twisted a long stem of grass between his fingers.

The woods were silent except for the occasional sounds drifting from the direction of the house. Mike and Ellie were playing in the swimming pool, supervised by Grace Nichols, David's mother, whom Leslie had finally met that morning in a brief, uncomfortably polite interlude, and by Mabel Baker, who looked after the house and family. The pool had been another surprise for Leslie, but she'd quickly realized the real need for it. In the water, Ellie was as agile and active as she was meant to be, not hampered by the slight limp Leslie had first witnessed that morning.

David looked over at her, gave her a fleeting smile, and resumed his silent study of the opposite creek bank and his own thoughts.

Why now? Leslie wondered as she felt the companionable ease of the morning slip from them. Not for hours had she felt the knot of tension gripping her. Not for hours had she been so full of insecurity.

But she knew why. Since those first few moments in the breakfast room, David had carried the responsibility of keeping the tension and insecurity at bay. Now he had fallen uncharacteristically silent and —

—and she didn't know whether it was uncharacteristic or not. She didn't know anything about him. Not really. Only what he'd chosen to tell her.

Stop it! she told herself. It was too late to back out

now. Or was it? What would he do if she simply said, *I've changed my mind. I can't go through with this.*

She watched sunlight and shadow moving across David, accenting then softening his features. He had high cheekbones and firm, smooth skin, now sun-darkened but with an underlying copper hue—gifts from his mother's grandmother, she knew, part Choctaw, and an early settler in this land which must have been even more wild and alien then . . . dark eyes, long dark lashes, lightly tipped with gold as the sunlight caught them, a straight nose that was perhaps a little too long, perhaps a little too arrogant, and his mouth, expressive when he talked, endearing when he smiled, sensual . . .

Leslie closed her eyes against the unbidden thoughts which assaulted her. Soon she would know too well how sensual David's mouth could be.

Almost against her will, she resumed her study of him. Thank God, he wasn't a giant. Too often in her life, she'd had to deal with men whose sheer size intimidated her. As it was, David was slightly over eight inches taller than her five-feet-two, and that was far enough for her to have to look up. She'd thought, when he first told her his weight, that he might be thin, but he wasn't. Lean, yes, but not thin. Sitting as he was, bent forward slightly, with his knees raised, the cotton cloth of his shirt strained against his shoulders and his jeans against his thighs, and Leslie saw the strength in muscle and sinew only accentuated, not hidden, by the fabric.

He was attractive—more than attractive, she amended—and more than she'd expected in her blind search for an escape. Successful, graceful in his movements, comfortable in his body, virile—she pulled her thoughts away from *that* track and concentrated on his face—and, it seemed, troubled by something. That much was evident by his posture and his expression.

Where are you, David? What thoughts are you lost in? But she couldn't ask him. She couldn't force herself to utter the words that would intrude on his privacy. He was a real person. For the first time that fact was brought home to her. He hadn't been before, she realized. In spite of her attempts at honesty, in spite of her belief that she had seen him as otherwise, he had remained slightly unreal, a stage character with whom she was acting out her very real drama. But he wasn't— could never again be—a stage character for her. He was a complex man, one with a successful career to contend with, family and friends to interact with, and memories as painful as hers.

What made her think she could live with this man as his wife? What made her think she could bring anything to him? What made her think she had any right to try?

"Do you think Mike will be happy here?" David spoke from the depths of his thoughts, without looking at her, yet making her remember what she could bring him and why she had to try: her son, the only reason she'd ever met David Nichols.

"Yes," she said. Then, aware of the tightness in her voice, she tried to soften her words. "That must have been some visit you had this morning. Mike seemed quite impressed with you."

A brief smile eased the tension of David's mouth. "Not with me so much as with the ranch. He'd never touched a horse before, never seen a new foal. But we got along together . . . fairly well, for strangers."

"And he and Ellie seem to . . ." Leslie's voice failed her. They were speaking so casually, yet of things that were the heart of their future, and all she could do was babble.

". . . get along as well as a boy and girl their ages can be expected to," David finished for her. "I suspect part of their rapport was caused by Mike seeing her as the old hand, someone who has a lot of new experiences for him, even though he might not want to admit it; but once the new has worn off, I hope they'll have found some common ground, a genuine affection for each other."

David turned gracefully, unexpectedly, until he faced her, and Leslie had the full force of his expression. "And you, Leslie? Will you be happy here?" he asked her, concerned, puzzled, and still troubled.

"I—I think so," she said, not knowing if it were true, not knowing anything but the spell his eyes were casting over her.

Hesitantly, he lifted his hands to cup her face and she felt the gentle abrasion of his thumbs as he traced them along her cheeks, her jaw, her lips.

This time there was no question in her mind. He was going to kiss her, Leslie knew, startlingly aware of their closeness and their isolation, and she wasn't sure she was ready for that. But as he hesitated, almost as if waiting for some sign from her, she also knew that she wanted to feel the touch of his mouth on hers, wanted to end the suspense that had settled over them, desperately needed to still the nerves clamoring within her for relief.

At least his hesitation disappeared as David claimed her mouth. For a moment Leslie stiffened against the unfamiliar intimacy, unsure of her own needs and unsure of how she should react to David's. Her hands fluttered helplessly before settling on his shoulders as she surrendered to the gentle persuasion of his mouth. His mouth—mobile, expressive, and, yes, she admitted, sensual.

Leslie felt the rough bark of the oak tree digging into her shoulders before David slid his hands behind her, protecting her from that abrasion, but there were so many other sensations...each one vivid, each one quickly joined by another: the feel of his firm shoulders under the sun-warmed fabric of his shirt; the clean, masculine scent with nothing artificial but the vaguely lingering aroma of soap; the velvet moistness of his tongue tracing her inner lips; the sound of her breathing, and his; the pounding of her heart, and his; the awakening of nerves long dormant; the awakening of hunger long dormant; her need, and his.

She felt his hands moving over her back, drawing her into the curve of his body. One hand slid down and around, resting on her ribs just below her breast. Although he made no move to touch her more intimately, she felt herself straining for his touch. Her heartbeat accelerated, beating in violent cadence. Her fingers twisted through the richness of his hair, tightened on his shoulder, and she arched closer, but still not able to be close enough. His tongue ceased its teasing, thrusting past her parted teeth to claim her mouth.

Leslie was only dimly aware of her moan as she surrendered her mouth to his possession, but David must have heard it. Slowly, reluctantly, he ended the kiss. He folded his arms around her and held Leslie against his chest, and she lay there quietly, not understanding how she'd responded so quickly, or why, just knowing that had David not pulled away, she might not have been able to.

He touched his fingers to her cheek, gazing down at her and looking almost as shaken as she felt. Once again her powers of speech had deserted her. With a sigh, she closed her eyes and rested her cheek against his heart. After a moment, he gave her a gentle hug and pulled away, rising gracefully to his feet and holding his hand out for her. "I think," he said, "it's time for us to head back to the house."

Phil Wilcox, David's cousin as well as his attorney, arrived shortly before three, looking less like a lawyer, Leslie thought, than anyone she had ever seen. She and David met with him in the comfortable downstairs study, the huge, strapping visitor dwarfing not only Leslie, but the room itself. He wore faded jeans, dusty boots, and a bright red knit shirt that clashed with his full red beard and shaggy mane of equally rich red hair. He clasped Leslie's hand, swallowing it in his firm grasp, and when he spoke, Leslie felt sure that no juror had ever slept through one of his arguments and that no spectator had ever strained to hear him from the back of a courtroom.

But Phil was amazingly considerate of her, kind, and courteous. David had told him what he'd told everyone else except his mother and the Bakers, who knew him too well for anything less than candid: that he and Leslie had known each other for some time, that for the past several months they'd been corresponding. It was more an evasion of the truth than a lie, David told her, but one he felt necessary in order to protect her from speculation until people could know her. Instead of diving right into business, Phil asked Leslie about herself and Mike and exchanged a few pleasantries with David. Only after she'd relaxed enough to laugh at one of his stories did he open his scuffed leather portfolio and drag out a sheaf of papers.

"Now both of you take a few minutes and read this," Phil said, handing each of them a copy of the papers.

Leslie looked hesitantly at David. "It's what we discussed—"

"It's what you discussed with David," Phil interrupted gruffly but not unkindly, "it's what he discussed with me, and it's what I discussed with that new-fangled typewriter in my office. Now what we have to see is if everybody understood each other." He smiled at Leslie. "It's for your own protection—both of you—but both of you are also giving up some rights, and I want to make sure you know that before I witness your signatures."

Chastised, Leslie sank back in her chair and began reading. Seeing it in writing made their agreement seem so cold, more like entering into a business arrangement than a marriage. David would adopt Mike, immediately

—that was the important thing, removing forever the risk that Harrison and Leta could take him from her. The rest of the provisions dealt with property settlement in case of divorce, or death. Leslie glanced anxiously toward David, but he was reading intently, a small frown creasing his brow. She turned back to the papers in her hand. It was a precaution, that was all. Each of them knew how unexpectedly death came. These provisions made more sense to her now that she'd seen his home, but she hadn't wanted any claim against him before coming out here, and she didn't now. She only wanted protection for Mike, which these papers, this marriage, guaranteed.

She continued reading, the legalese adding pages to what had once seemed so simple, until she reached the final paragraph. The agreement could be set aside if both of them agreed in writing to do so, and would be amended by the birth of a child after the first year. Leslie looked up questioningly to find David watching her.

"You've finished?" Phil asked.

Leslie nodded.

"Is it all right with you, Leslie?" David asked quietly. Was it? They had never discussed that last, surprising paragraph. David and Elaine had wanted more children, she knew that. She herself had wanted more children, he knew that. But somehow she'd never projected those wants into this marriage. She would be mothering his nine-year-old daughter, and that was as far as she'd carried it. Did she want to bear his child as well? Was he asking her to? Or was this some sort of escape clause Phil had insisted upon?

"The way this is written, we have a year to think about it," David added, acknowledging her questions but not answering them.

Think about it? Yes, she could do that. Leslie found a smile for him, nodded and reached for a pen.

"Damn fools." Phil's words stopped her. "When

David first came to me about this agreement, I thought it was probably the smart thing to do, considering his circumstances. But the more I talked to him, the more I began to wonder. I do a lot of these agreements, more than you'd expect in this county, and I give a standard lecture with each one, which you're going to get now. It seems to me, if you are planning to get married and bring children into this world, you need a lot more going for you than a legal agreement telling you how you're going to divide everything up when you fail. You need trust, in each other and in what you're doing, and no piece of paper is going to give you that."

"I trust David," Leslie said quickly. "I wouldn't be here if I didn't."

Phil pinned her with a long, steadying gaze. "No," he said finally. "I don't suppose you would be. And he trusts you, to a point, which leads me to think that there's something neither of you is telling me."

Like what? Leslie thought. Like the fact that they hadn't even seen each other until last night? Like the fact that they trusted each other enough this far but didn't know each other well enough to know how long that trust could last? Their marriage would be forever, she had promised that much, a real marriage, based on friendship, respect, and, yes, trust. A marriage lacking in only one element—love.

"There's nothing, Phil," David said firmly. "Nothing important."

Phil ran his hand through his beard, rubbing his jaw. "Okay," he said, sighing. He turned to Leslie. "This agreement is as fair to both of you as I could make it, given what I had to work with. You can have another lawyer look at it before you sign it, if you want to."

"That won't be necessary." Leslie smiled at Phil and picked up her pen with a show of more confidence than she felt. She glanced over at David, who held his pen positioned over the paper. He seemed to draw himself back from his thoughts, but before he could turn and catch her watching him and wondering where those thoughts were going, she lowered her head and signed her name.

Leslie left the two men as they walked toward Phil's car, engaged in conversation. Amazing, she thought, as she closed the front door and started up the short flight of stairs. A few moments before, Phil had been lawyer and Dutch-uncle lecturer. Now, they were talking about David's limited veterinarian practice, and Phil was seeking David's advice on his growing herd of registered Santa Gertrudis cattle as though no sharp words had been spoken.

Leslie still clutched her copy of the agreement. She didn't want to think about it but couldn't help herself. She did trust David. *She did*. She had to, to bring him the most important thing in her life. Phil had left with the rest of the information he needed to draw up Mike's adoption papers. And David trusted her with Ellie. Leslie stopped at the head of the stairs. He trusted her to care for Ellie, not to adopt her. That subject had never been brought up, not by David, and not even by Phil, who had certainly not hesitated to bulldoze his way through emotional issues that were a lot more sensitive than that.

"Has Phil left?"

Grace Nichols stood at the door to the breakfast room, frowning slightly.

Leslie looked up at the woman. She was several inches taller than Leslie. But, Leslie thought, almost everyone was several inches taller than she was. That in itself shouldn't be intimidating. She had short, light brown hair, liberally laced with gray, and with that well-tended look obtainable only with regular visits to a beautician. Her face also showed a well-tended appearance and the signs of graceful aging.

Leslie felt her muscles tighten. "He and David are outside, talking."

Mrs. Nichols glanced at the paper in Leslie's hand. "You're going ahead with it, then?"

Oh, Lord, she didn't need this now. Not a replay of the disapproval Leta Burgess had voiced every time she spoke to her. Not now, when her own doubts were magnifying by the minute.

"Yes," Leslie said tightly, walking past the other woman.

"Leslie."

Leslie stopped at the soft command and turned to face David's mother.

"Have I done something to offend you?"

Had she? Leta Burgess had certainly never missed an opportunity to remind Leslie that she'd had the lack of good manners to become pregnant at fifteen, that Michael had been forced to give up what would have been a brilliant medical career to marry her. Leta never acknowledged that the real reason Michael had dropped out of medical school had been the withdrawal of the Burgesses' financial support—money that before his marriage his parents had been more than willing to provide. And even though she didn't know all that had happened that last night, when Michael had unwittingly stumbled into an armed robbery at the neighborhood grocery, Leta still managed to blame Leslie for his death.

But David's mother knew none of those things. Had done none of those things. She had been nothing but unfailingly polite in what must certainly be a painful situation for her.

"No," Leslie said, sighing softly. "I'm sorry. I know you don't approve."

"It's not that I don't approve," Mrs. Nichols told her. "I don't *understand*. But any arguing I'm going to do about this marriage has already been done. I've raised my son to make his own decisions, and I stand by him in those decisions. Be a good wife for him, Leslie, and I'll never give you any reason to think I disapprove of you."

Mrs. Nichols's promise was so much more than she'd expected that Leslie felt a small flare of hope. There were so many similarities between David's mother and Leta. Both women had been extremely beautiful in their youth, both were meticulously groomed, both secure in the money and social position and power which stood behind them.

"Thank you," Leslie said, wanting to believe what the woman said, but unable to accept her words without reservation. "I intend to do my best."

And David intended to do his best to be a good husband for her. Leslie did accept that. She only hoped that between the two of them, their best would be enough.

Chapter

3

"Do you, Leslie, take David to be your lawfully wedded husband, to love, honor, and cherish . . ."

David looked down at the slender figure standing beside him. Leslie's head was bowed slightly, and the sunlight streaming through the unshaded windows cast red and gold highlights on the soft amber waves veiling her face and falling gracefully over her shoulders. But even without seeing her expression, he thought he knew the awareness that held her still and subdued.

Formalities, he had called this ceremony, and that's how he'd thought of it—until the moment he'd taken her hand as his cousin Ben Wilcox, a slighter and less flamboyant version of Phil, still wearing his judge's robes from the afternoon court docket, began reciting with quiet dignity the promises that would forever bind them together. They were, David thought, promises he had never imagined he would make to another woman, promises he knew they both meant to keep—that is, with one notable exception.

He wasn't lying, he convinced himself. He could love Leslie, for her gentleness, for her courage, for her loyalty. He just couldn't... *love* her. But standing beside her, surrounded by the small group of his close family and friends, David wondered again if it was going to be enough.

At least he was surrounded by family and friends, he realized. It seemed right for Hank to be standing beside him. Hank had been his father's closest friend and had been standing beside David for as long as he could remember. But Leslie had met Mabel only two days before. She was among strangers for one of the most important moments of her life—strangers except for Mike, who stood to one side of them, looking as solemn and awed by the proceedings as did Ellie.

David felt Leslie's hand tremble in his. Carefully, meaning only to give her some of the strength he was pretending to feel, he squeezed her hand. He felt the barest return of pressure before she looked up at him and smiled. The smile transformed her face, chasing away the shadows that he'd seen lurking in her eyes.

"I do," she said with soft determination.

David unlocked the door and pushed it open while Leslie waited in the shadows of approaching night on the porch beside him. She'd been silent since they'd left the children with his mother at the restaurant, and somewhere between parking his Buick in the drive and inserting his key in the front door, he seemed to have lost his voice, as well.

Did Leslie expect a romantic gesture? Would he be a hypocrite if he lifted her over the threshold? Taking the decision from him, Leslie walked past him into the hall-

way. The house was dark except for one soft light in the
living area. Hesitating for only a moment, Leslie
walked down the stairs toward the light, and David followed her, chuckling when he saw what awaited them
on the coffee table.

"I should have known we couldn't leave those two
women in the house this afternoon without them planning some surprise," he said.

Leslie walked to the table and stood looking down at
the small, beautifully decorated cake and the pile of
white and silver wrapped boxes. "There's a note," she
said in a tight little voice.

David glanced briefly at the envelope propped on the
table before the tension in Leslie's voice penetrated and
he turned his attention to her. She was beautiful in the
softly draped blue dress that seemed to float around her,
but right now she seemed more like a guest in his home
than someone who had promised to live there with
him—a guest who wasn't sure of her welcome.

He plucked the note from the table and handed it to
her. "You open it," he suggested, "while I get comfortable." He shrugged out of his suit jacket and loosened
his tie before walking to the patio doors and opening
them, letting the night breeze and the distant, lonely cry
of a whippoorwill into the room. "Do you want to take
off your shoes or change clothes?" he asked casually,
turning to watch her as the light bathed her in a golden
glow.

"No, I—" She held the note out toward him.

What had happened to her? This wasn't the woman
he had come to know over the past few months. That
woman had met unemployment and financial disaster
and emotional blackmail with a calm and unwavering
courage. "Go ahead," he said, careful not to let any of
what he was thinking creep into his voice. "It has your
name on it, too."

"Yes, it does." Leslie sounded as though that surprised her, but she opened the envelope and unfolded the single sheet of note paper. She looked up at him, and this time he had no doubt about her surprise. It was evident in her stunned expression. "Your mother says . . ."

"Go on." He smiled wryly. "Surely my mother didn't miss an opportunity to leave me a few words of wisdom."

"No, she didn't." Swallowing once, Leslie began reading, her voice gaining strength, then losing it. "David and Leslie, since you won't take time for a honeymoon, at least accept the gift of privacy. Hank and Mabel will not intrude on your time together, nor will they let anyone else, until I bring the children home Monday morning. Love, your meddling mother."

David choked back a laugh and hoped Leslie was not aware of its harshness. Meddling was right. He and Leslie needed privacy, needed time together, but unless something happened to knock down the wall between them, he wasn't sure how they could fill almost a week.

"That's it?" he asked as lightly as possible.

"Except for a P.S.," Leslie said, attempting a smile and almost succeeding. "Look in the downstairs fridge."

Tender touch, David remembered, walking toward her. It was amazing how touch sometimes gentled a frightened animal. And he wanted to touch Leslie, he realized. Wanted to. Needed to. The thought shook him, but he draped his arm lightly over her shoulder. "Then let's go look," he said, guiding her across the room. "Knowing my mother, anything could be waiting for us."

The downstairs refrigerator was in a room tucked into a corner of the huge den, which filled almost the entire area under the bedroom wing. Elaine had called it her "play" kitchen. She had loved to entertain, and from that kitchen she'd prepared countless buffet suppers and presided over a room filled with laughter and sophisticated, free-flowing conversation. The room was silent now, and dark, and the oversized refrigerator which David hurriedly opened was empty except for two tulip glasses and a napkin-wrapped bottle of champagne.

"How nice," Leslie said, breaking the hushed silence. "I haven't had champagne in years."

Nice, David thought, suppressing a sigh, and now, although he never depended upon alcohol as a crutch, needed. Maybe, just maybe, it would relax them enough to get them through the evening, but if not, it would at least help fill the time and keep the ghosts at bay—his and Leslie's. He hooked his fingers around the glasses and lifted the bottle, urging Leslie with a nod and a smile to return to the light, to leave the room where, for a moment, his memories had taken on more reality than the woman at his side.

Eventually, as they shared the cake, sipping champagne and opening the waiting boxes, Leslie slipped off her shoes and tucked her feet beneath her on the long white couch which circled the coffee table. With his arm stretched along the back of it, David relaxed back into the depths of the couch, enjoying the excitement she tried to hide at opening each package and the emotions that played across her expressive features in spite of the weariness steadily claiming her.

The gifts had all borne her name, and David cursed himself silently for not thinking of a wedding present himself when he saw how much pleasure she received from even the simplest of them.

Mabel had chosen to be practical, as Mabel would, but even David recognized the care that she'd taken when Leslie opened a small box and found an array of his favorite recipes painstakingly copied onto decorative index cards. His mother, practical in another vein, had taken the opportunity to give Leslie things of a more personal nature.

Leslie held the last box in her lap, carefully unfolding the tissue which hid its contents. Hearing her soft exclamation, he returned his attention to her as she held up a nightgown and matching robe in peach-colored satin. He watched her hands tremble slightly as she stroked the delicate fabric, a faint flush coloring her cheeks . . . her eyes unusually bright.

Was she offended by the blatantly sensual nature of the gift? He lifted his arm from the back of the sofa and cupped her shoulder with his hand, trying to banish the vision of her small, firm body draped in the caressing satin. "She meant well," he offered.

Leslie gave him a tentative smile. "I believe she did." Sighing, she leaned back and turned her head on his arm, facing him. "It's real, isn't it? It's done."

At that moment, it seemed right for him to tighten his arm around her and draw her against his body, to lift his hand to her face before tracing a path along her throat. He did neither. Silently he added what he suspected she meant, what had become more apparent in the last two days than all her words before her arrival had been able to convey: *You and Mike are safe*. But as he tried to find a way to convey that to her, her lids fluttered down to veil her eyes from him, her breathing deepened, she relaxed against his arm, and David realized with dismay that both his words and his actions would have to wait. She was asleep.

Without the animation of her expression to distract him, the shadows beneath her eyes were more obvious, as was a hint of sharpness about her features that bespoke the strain she'd been under and a weight loss she hadn't needed. Even in repose a small frown marred her brow. He didn't doubt that she was exhausted. He knew the past few days had been emotionally wearing on him, and she'd had less than a week since making the definite decision to close her apartment, and tie up all the loose ends of her life in New Jersey, and come to him.

And she'd had all those weeks before that, weeks she'd admitted were grim, although he now knew she hadn't expressed just how grim they really had been. Only Mike had let that slip.

She should have told him, David thought, instead of letting him be lulled by her optimism about up-coming job interviews and her assertions that her dwindling savings were still sufficient for her needs.

There was a lot of pride wrapped up in that small body, David thought, gazing down at Leslie, unwilling to move or disturb her. It hadn't been money that had brought her to him or precipitated their decision, hurling them together faster than either of them had planned. It had been Harrison and Leta Burgess's final ultimatum to sue for Mike's custody if she did not give him up voluntarily and without a fight.

As he watched, Leslie's frown deepened and a small sound escaped her. Shifting slightly, he moved closer to her. A lot of pride, he thought, as she turned to him, resting her head on his shoulder and one small fist against his heart, a lot of loyalty, and a lot of love. He had seen the love she had to give in her reaction to Ellie and Ellie's response to her in the short time she'd been here, and in her interaction with Mike.

And here it was his wedding night. A strange ending to an even stranger day, he thought as he sat in the darkened room cradling her slight weight against him, listening to the plaintive cry of the whippoorwill, feeling the caress of the evening breeze, the tantalizing rise and fall of Leslie's breasts against him, and the soft fanning of her breath against his throat. And he wanted her, not just her body—the yearning was nebulous, less than half formed—although he knew his physical need was now more than just an aching loneliness.

Leslie stirred against him in her sleep and again that

small sound escaped her lips. A dream? he wondered. If
so, it didn't appear to be a pleasant one. He lifted his
hand to her face and smoothed her hair back from her
cheek.

She opened her eyes slowly, confused, but she didn't
pull away from him. "I'm sorry. I must have—"

He placed his fingers on her lips and shook his head.
"It's all right."

He slipped his arm from around her, rose, and turned
to lift her from the sofa. "Bedtime," he said softly.

She covered a yawn with her hand, then nodded, letting him help her to her feet. "Do you know the problem
with a big house?" she asked sleepily, and he wondered
if she were truly awake. "The room you're in is always
so far away from the one you're going to."

David chuckled and draped his arm around her, turning her from her misguided direction and leading her to
the stairs that led directly to the bedroom wing.

He hadn't meant to stop at her room. Some assump-
tions had been made by both of them; one he had made
was that Leslie would be sharing his bed, that night and
every night in the future, but when they reached her
doorway, he found that he couldn't lead her any further.
She would go with him; he was sure of that much. He
knew that if he led her the few feet down the hallway to
his room, she would go with him and submit to whatever he wanted. Sometime during the evening she had
lost her uneasiness with him. Either that, or she was
half dead on her feet and still locked in sleep.

Whatever the reason, David knew he didn't want
Leslie *submitting* to anything.

She looked up at him in confusion when he halted at
her door and turned her in his arms. He wanted to pull
her against him, to feel again the pressure of her breasts
against his chest, to feel her warm and compliant in his
arms, to feel her mouth, soft and giving, beneath his.

Instead he planted a light kiss on her forehead and released her. "Get some sleep," he said.

He hoped she'd sleep, because as he watched her hesitate and then walk into the bedroom alone, he knew he wouldn't be able to.

He wanted her, he admitted as he lay alone in his bed, but he wanted more than just a compliant body beneath him. His fleeting thoughts from earlier in the evening swirled around him. He wanted the warmth of the love she offered Ellie, showered on Mike—but he'd never asked for that, had no right to expect it, and wasn't sure he could accept it, if offered. No. What he wanted was the woman he'd come to know through letters and telephone calls. The one who had shared her hopes and dreams with him and had beguiled him into remembering half-forgotten dreams of his own. The one who had helped him remember how to laugh. That was what he wanted. That woman, coming to him willingly, not because it was expected of her.

Sharing his thoughts and emotions had not been easy for David—there were things he doubted he would ever be able to tell anyone—but the anonymity of the first few letters had helped, and then Leslie had simply refused to let him do otherwise once they began talking. He realized that she'd carried most of the burden in their crash course in intimacy. He realized, too, that she wasn't able right now to continue to carry that burden. It was up to him, he knew. He could either let their early attempts at openness stagnate, or he could assume some of the responsibility for continuing them . . . but David wasn't sure if he was any more able than Leslie was to do that . . . or if he'd ever be.

The glow from the hallway only backlit the figure moving toward her bed in the shadowy darkness; it didn't illuminate it. Leslie came awake quickly, frightened and disoriented by the strange placement of the bed and the door until she remembered where she was and heard the reassuring sound of David's voice as he seated himself beside her. "Leslie, wake up," he said softly.

Leaning forward, he set something on the nightstand next to the bed, and Leslie smelled the tempting aroma of coffee before he switched on the bedside lamp and she had to close her eyes against its glare.

And then she remembered that the sky was still pitch black outside the windows. She sat up in bed, drawing the sheet with her. "Is something wrong?"

David was already shaved, showered, and dressed, and for a moment he seemed puzzled by her question. He chuckled, shook his head, and handed her the coffee cup. "No," he said. "Nothing's wrong. I want to show you something."

Her fear was gone, but now she was puzzled. "In the middle of the night?"

"No. At the beginning of morning."

Leslie had only vague memories of falling asleep on the sofa, dreamlike recollections of the walk to her room and her confusion when he'd left her there, alone. Now it was morning? She caught his wrist with the hand that wasn't occupied with the coffee cup and turned it so that she could see his watch. She groaned when she saw the time, but along with the realization that he was awakening her earlier than she'd ever intentionally been awake before came the realization that he hadn't pushed her for physical intimacy even though she'd expected him to, even though she'd been . . . prepared for it.

"Sadist," she said with exaggerated mock disgust. "You told me you were a morning person, but this is ridiculous."

"And also unusual, even for me," he admitted, smiling. "Get up and get dressed. We don't have much time."

"Time for what?"

"I can't tell you; you have to see it to believe it."

"Okay," she said, leaning back against the headboard and sipping her coffee. It was wonderful, just the way she liked it, fresh and strong. "Maybe this will work instead. Dressed for what?"

"Jeans," he told her, maddeningly supplying the necessary information without answering her question. "A long-sleeved shirt. I don't suppose you have any boots?"

"Fleece lined with two-inch heels—back in New Jersey in a box in Madge's closet. But I don't think that's what you meant anyway, is it?"

He shook his head, and his mouth curved in amusement. He lifted his hand, and Leslie realized she was still holding his wrist. He carried her hand with him while he brushed the hair from her cheek. "You're beautiful in the morning. Do you know that? Even if you can't talk without caffeine." Their joined hands trailed down her jaw. . .

"Sensible shoes, then," he said, suddenly breaking the contact and rising. "Meet me downstairs in no more than ten minutes." He paused at the doorway. "I have your second cup of coffee waiting in a thermos bottle."

After David left, Leslie took another sip of coffee and stared reflectively at the dark liquid in the cup. Something had just happened between them. She wasn't sure exactly *what*, but this was more the way she had envisioned their interacting: relaxed, at ease with each other, even teasing. That was the way it had been since the first few letters. She didn't understand the change, but then she didn't understand her discomfort of the past few days. Maybe she'd been more tightly strung than she'd thought. He certainly hadn't done anything to cause her unease. David was just—well, in spite of being so much more than she had expected, David was still David: kind, sensitive, and caring. Maybe she had been suffering from pre-wedding jitters. Maybe she—

She suddenly heard the sound of a car engine and realized that minutes had passed. Lifting the cup to her lips, she took a long sustaining sip before sighing and swinging her legs over the edge of the bed. Maybe she'd better get dressed and go see whatever it was he wanted to show her at this god-awful hour of the morning.

David had brought a jeep up to the front door—that was the engine she'd heard—and had already placed a thermos and a folded blanket on the floor of the passenger side when he lifted her up onto the seat.

There was nothing but the sound of the jeep's engine to break the silence of the night, nothing but the jeep's headlights to illuminate what at times seemed little more than a path winding upward through the trees in the eerie darkness. Leslie clutched the rail on the dash in front of her as the jeep's tires bounced off a rougher than usual place in the trail, holding tight to steady herself, trusting that David knew where he was going and why. But she had to admit that heading out toward an unknown destination in the pre-dawn darkness with David was exhilarating; that the newness of the experience, as well as the cool early morning air, had done more to dispel the residue of her sleep-fogged thoughts and actions than caffeine ever had.

David drove for several minutes, then stopped the jeep and killed the engine. "Now we have to walk a short distance," he told her. "Watch your step."

"David," she said laughing, "I can't *see* my step." Though that wasn't quite true. The darkness was fading. Now she could discern vague shapes within the shadows.

David laughed with her, and when he helped her down and lifted the thermos and blanket from the floor, he looped his free arm around her waist. "Okay. *I'll* watch your step," he told her, guiding her along and up a narrow path.

After a short distance, the path leveled and widened,

then disappeared altogether in the grasses of a small meadow still cloaked in shadow. David led her unerringly across the meadow to an even darker area in the thick, dry grass and stopped.

"Stand right there," he said softly, releasing her to spread the blanket on what seemed to be a large, flat rock. "There's a drop-off about two feet in front of you." He shook out the blanket, positioned it, knelt, and reached for her hand. "Now we sit."

Leslie lowered herself beside him. He shook his head, turning her and guiding her until they sat at the very edge of the drop-off.

"Sit?" she asked. ". . . and do what?"

"Watch," he told her quietly. "Listen. And feel."

Watch, when there was nothing but darkness? Listen to nothing but silence? The cool morning air penetrated her shirt, and Leslie shivered. Without speaking, David put his arm around her, drawing her into the warmth of his body. The gray now was dissolving; shapes were becoming more distinct. And the silence—she heard first the breeze ruffling the leaves and grasses behind her, then the early morning call of a bird, and an answering trill. They were facing a mountain ridge. Below them she could make out the shape of a wide, sloping ledge, and then another drop-off, and below that what appeared to be a high, cleared valley.

There were cattle grazing below them; she could see their shapes in the shadow that was now becoming more rose than gray. A wide band of trees meandered through the valley, marking the path of what appeared to be a large stream. From that stream she saw a pale, sinuous cloud rising and spreading pink-hued softness over the valley floor until the cattle, distinct now in the growing light, seemed to be walking through the cloud and grazing on its ephemeral substance.

Leslie listened as the forest awoke behind her, watched spellbound as the world came alive before her eyes, growing in detail and structure but still rose-colored and magical, as the sunrise, mauve and blue and gray and orange and so many other colors she gave up trying to identify them but glowing with a gentleness never seen in sunset, crept over the mountain and gave birth to a new morning.

She sighed in contentment and relaxed against David. Now she knew what he had meant when he'd told her to feel. "It was beautiful," she whispered, for whispering seemed right. "I feel whole, rejuvenated somehow. At peace."

"I hoped you would." He tightened his arm around her, holding her even closer, and for a moment Leslie felt that their closeness was more than physical. "Cold?" he asked.

She shook her head. "Not now."

"Do you remember the park you told me about in Paterson? The place you used to go when you had a problem to work out or just needed to be . . . with yourself for a while?"

She nodded, knowing instinctively what he was going to tell her.

"This is the place I pictured when you told me about yours. This land had been in my mother's family for years, until they lost it. Mom's grandmother was born in a cabin just a few feet behind us. The cabin has been gone for years, but every spring, jonquils and iris outline where it once stood. My dad bought this land with the proceeds from his first gas well because he knew how much my mother loved the mountains, and I found the homesite when I was— oh, no more than nine, exploring where I shouldn't have been. It's been a special place for me ever since, somewhere I could come to think, to let myself feel . . . to heal. And last year, when Ellie had to go back for more surgery and we still didn't know whether she would ever walk again, I found that I didn't have to come here physically; just knowing it was here, waiting, helped.

"I think what I'm trying to say is that I want you to know this place is here if you ever need it, Leslie."

He'd been holding her all this time, but now Leslie turned, sliding her arms around him. Why had she worried? She and David had more going for them than most people ever found in a marriage. It would be enough—more than enough.

Chapter
4

"OKAY," LESLIE MUTTERED, "one more time." She blew the hair out of her eyes and looked at the brown giant who stared back at her with placid interest. She drew in a deep breath and lifted her arms to grasp the saddle with both hands.

"Not like that."

She felt David behind her, close enough that she was aware of the smooth coordination of his actions and the heat from his body as he reached around her, loosening the grip she had with her right hand on the back of the saddle. "That's a good way to get kicked."

"Kicked?" she asked, releasing her grasp and attempting to step away only to find herself trapped in the warm prison of David's arms. "This horse is going to kick?"

She felt David's chuckle and the fanning of his breath across her cheek before he stepped back, putting inches of space between them. "Henry? Henry hasn't kicked anything in close to ten years. But there are horses who will, and it's best for you to learn from the start how to protect yourself."

Learn. That was what it was all about, Leslie reminded herself. No one expected her to be an expert rider when she had never even been on a horse. Ellie had learned. David was sure that Mike would have no trouble learning. There was no reason why she couldn't learn to ride a horse—if she could only manage to get *on* the blasted thing.

"Here," David said, positioning her hands. "One hand on his neck. One on the pommel. Then put your left foot in the stirrup."

Leslie twisted around from her awkward position to look at him over her shoulder. "This isn't going to work," she said, shaking her head. "I have long legs for a short person, and I'm relatively agile, but I'm not a contortionist."

David smiled, the lazy smile she was beginning to recognize, the one that only began to reveal the humor in his eyes. "I think you may be right, " he said. "Tell you what. Because this is Henry, and until you get used to mounting, let's try it with both hands on the pommel." He lifted her hand from Henry's neck and positioned it with her other one on the knob jutting up from the front of the saddle, while Leslie wondered, was it her imagination, or did he stand a little closer to her than necessary? Did his hand linger on hers a little longer than need be?

"Okay," he said, backing away from her to give her room to move. "Try it again."

Once again Leslie drew in a deep breath, this time not knowing if she needed it for the effort facing her, or because her heart had stopped while David was holding her. She nodded and concentrated on getting herself up onto Henry's broad back. This time, with the help of a jump that had been totally ineffective before, she managed to hook her toe in the stirrup and lift herself up.

The heat of the day, combined with her exertion, rose around her like a sauna, and Leslie found it almost impossible to believe that only a few hours before she'd actually felt chilled. Now sweat—maybe "ladies don't sweat, they perspire," but this felt anything but ladylike —beaded on her face, molded her shirt damply to her back, and trickled between her breasts. She hung onto the pommel, her body pressed precariously against Henry's left side.

Turning her head to give David a triumphant little grin, she wondered why she was feeling so proud of herself for clinging to a hunk of creaking leather atop a smelly four-legged animal in 100-degree-plus weather with the sun stealing whatever moisture her skin had left to feed the sultry air around them.

David's smile was her answer. "Good!" he said encouragingly. "Now swing your right leg over."

Leslie did, landing with a thump in the saddle. Then she looked down, and down, at the hard-packed earth of the corral that seemed dozens of feet beneath her, and suddenly wished she hadn't. She swallowed once and clutched the pommel even more tightly, but David didn't seemed concerned, at least not about her falling. He walked around the horse and checked the stirrups, while giving her instructions in his soft, slow voice, and positioning her with his fleeting yet sure touch—his hands on her waist, scooting her back in the saddle; on her foot, showing her where the ball of her foot should balance; on her thigh and calf, flexing her knee to the right position.

Leslie looked down at David, much more interested in him than in the distance between her and the ground. All she could see was the top of his cowboy hat as he bent to make some adjustment to the left stirrup. She wondered again, had his hands lingered on her thigh a bit longer than necessary? Was he trying to make her aware of him? If so, she admitted, he was succeeding with an ease that surprised her, but when he looked up at her, his expression was guileless.

"Ready for your first ride?" he asked.

Leslie saw nothing in his eyes but polite interest and she determined he would see in hers nothing of the unreasonable fear she was feeling. She couldn't force herself to release her death grip on the pommel, but she could manage her voice. "Sure," she said lightly.

David glanced at her white knuckles and then at her fixed smile. "Relax," he told her. "You're going to feel like you've been beaten if you try to ride like that."

A lot of things in Leslie's life had seemed to be trying to spin out of control. She had always held onto the conviction that they couldn't, unless she let them, but when she felt her body sway and jolt with Henry's first step, she knew that she was completely helpless, at the mercy of more than a thousand pounds of strange horse and of the man who was leading him.

Relax? she thought as she took another bone-rattling jolt. *Not in this lifetime.* But even as she was denying that she ever could, she began to do just that. David wouldn't have put her in danger; she knew him well enough to believe that.

"Dad didn't ride until after he moved here and married Mom," David told her as he led Henry in a wide circle. "Then he decided that, being a rancher, he ought to be a horseman, too. There are still places, at least on this part of the ranch, where you can't take even a jeep; there were lots more of them then. But he took one look at the working stock Hank had acquired and said, no way. Power, speed, and handling ability were all right for a sports car but not for any four-legged animal he had to balance himself on the back of. He had only two requirements for his horse: Since he was a big man, the horse had to be big, and it had to be comfortable—sort of like a big rocking chair.

"So after two or three other horses that didn't quite meet the second requirement, Hank finally found him Henry, and trained him for Dad. I never heard the story behind Henry's name, but knowing my dad and Hank and what close friends they were, I suspect there is one."

Leslie would never have compared Henry to a rocking chair, but she found that once she stopped resisting the horse's motion and surrendered to it, the punishing jolting stopped as well. And while the sun was every bit as merciless as it had been when she'd fought her way onto Henry's back, their movement around the corral stirred the air and brought her some relief from the sweltering heat.

David halted Henry and looked up at her. "That wasn't so bad, was it?"

"No," Leslie admitted. She looked at her hands. They still held the pommel, but at least now they didn't grip it.

"Ready to take control?"

"Control?" The word squeaked out in a shocked whisper as Leslie felt her expression melting.

David laughed and patted her foot. "Kick free of this stirrup."

She did, reflexively, not knowing what to expect, and a moment later, with only the shifting and creaking of the saddle to warn her, David swung himself up behind her.

"Sit up straight," he told her as he reached around her.

Leslie did and felt herself enveloped by him. Her heart gave a funny little catch and then thudded into overdrive. Her back was pressed against his chest, her legs molded to his, her arms defined by his as he reached over her, and what little part of her was not actually touched by him was tinglingly alive.

"These are the reins," David said, bending his head so that she felt the whisper of his breath against her ear when he spoke.

"What?" Leslie knew that she ought to listen, but she wasn't sure she was capable of concentrating on what he was telling her.

"The reins," David repeated. "With these, you tell the horse which direction to turn—"

"Like a steering wheel," Leslie murmured, trying to find something familiar to focus on. The furious, immediate response of her body, the new emotions, the questions, the doubts, and now, for the first time with David, an anticipation that was swirling about her—certainly none of these signposts were familiar.

David chuckled, and Leslie felt the ripple of his chest through her shirt, through her flesh.

"And brakes," he said, "and other things. But remember, it's *power* steering and power brakes, so you need a light touch. Otherwise you can hurt the horse—and yourself."

The idea of her being able to hurt something the size of Henry, even accidentally, was so novel it was almost enough to restore her concentration. Almost, that is, until David lifted her wrists from the pommel and pressed the narrow leather reins into her fingers, then closed his hands over hers. She controlled the horse; that was the message his actions showed her, but he controlled her—controlled her in a way he gave no sign of being aware of.

They were moving. Somehow, with a flick of his wrist, David had activated Henry's slow, forward motion, and each of the horse's ponderous steps only made her more aware of David's taut body pressed against hers.

Leslie had never thought of horseback riding as being

an erotic activity; it was something cowboys and Indians did in movies, but she knew she would never again be able to watch a western without remembering this afternoon. Could David tell how she felt? Was he going through the same rush of sensations as she was? Was it the thud of his heartbeat she felt racing through her where her back melded into his chest or was it only the echo of her own?

"Now a right turn," David said in the same easy, matter-of-fact voice he had used with her since the riding lesson began. With a barely perceptible pressure of his hand on hers, Leslie felt Henry veer to the right. "And a left." As Henry ambled to the left Leslie swayed with his motion, balancing herself, aware of the slide of denim against denim where her thigh rested against David's, of the pressure of her shoulder against his.

"And a stop." David eased back the reins, halting Henry, then brought their hands to rest on the pommel.

No, Leslie thought, sitting there embraced by him more thoroughly than if he had deliberately taken her in his arms, she wasn't alone in her feelings or her awareness—she couldn't be. But other than a slight tightening of his arms on hers, David gave no indication that he was anything but a teacher exercising a great deal of patience with a new and somewhat shy pupil.

"Now it's your turn," he said, loosening his light grasp but leaving his hands on hers.

Leslie drew in a lungful of air. This time she had no question about why she'd forgotten to breathe, and it had nothing to do with fear of Henry. Her movements were jerky, without the grace of David's, but Henry began moving.

"Good," David said encouragingly. "Now a right. Easy. Easy. Now a left. That's fine. Now stop."

She pulled back on the reins. Miraculously, Henry halted. She rested their still joined hands on the pommel. She wanted to lean back against David, to surrender at least momentarily to the tension that gripped her, but without some sign from him, some indication that he shared and even welcomed what she felt, she couldn't. So she sat very straight, very still, with his arms around her just grazing the sides of her breasts as they moved gently with the exertion of breathing, and waited.

"I think that's . . . enough for today."

David's terse words jarred her back to the reality of the baked clay ground of the corral, the barns shimmering in the afternoon heat, her clothes clinging damply to her.

As quickly and easily as David had mounted behind her, he dismounted, reached for the reins, and patted Henry's massive neck, leaving Leslie feeling alone, light-headed, awkward, and foolish. Of course he hadn't shared the need that had surprised her, that had almost overpowered her. How could he have? Elaine had been a beautiful woman, had ridden almost before she could walk. While Leslie—Leslie forced a wry smile to her lips, trying not to let any of her emotions show. Right now she felt about as attractive as the proverbial wet dishrag, and as far as horsemanship went, she barely knew the difference between giddap and whoa. It must have been painful for David, drawing comparisons between her and Elaine and realizing the inadequacies of the woman he was now married to, but no more painful than it was for her to recognize the truth of her situation. She was second choice, an imitation wife because he was still tied to the memory of a woman who'd been dead for more than two years, and while he might be willing to commit his life, his home, even his child to her, his heart was definitely off limits.

David looked up at her. His expression revealed none of his thoughts, and Leslie hoped her own was as bland, as pleasant, as seemingly open. "I think I need one more lesson," she said as lightly as she could.

He cocked an eyebrow inquiringly.

"How do I get down?"

Any hope that he might lift her down, hold her against himself, do something—anything—to dispell the pall of gloomy thoughts that had settled over her faded with his slow smile.

"Do you remember how you got up there?" he asked.

Leslie laughed in spite of her mood. "There are some things people are destined never to forget."

His soft laugh joined hers, and he was still smiling when he took Henry firmly by the neck, holding him steady. "Good. Then all you have to do is reverse the procedure."

Leslie grimaced at him, took a long look at the ground below, then glanced back at David. "Sure," she said with as much bravado as she could muster. "Nothing to it."

And there wasn't, not really, except for a moment of awkwardness as once again she clung to Henry's side before kicking free and landing with enough force to knock the air from her lungs and rock her back on her heels. She recovered her breath and her balance and, for the first time in several minutes, looked *up* at David, determined that he would never know the thoughts that had rocked her every bit as much as the jump down had. He had been honest with her; it wasn't his fault that only one day after their marriage she wanted to rail against the terms of a contract she had so readily agreed to. She dusted her hands together and shot him a cocky grin. "Piece of cake."

"Sounds good to me," he said, deliberately misconstruing her words and her intent. "And iced tea. About a gallon of it. But first, let's take care of Henry." He eased between her and the horse and began unbuckling and loosening straps.

"*I'll* take care of Henry."

Leslie turned toward the flatly drawled voice. Hank

Baker had lived up to Grace Nichols's promise that he wouldn't intrude on their privacy. Leslie had seen him earlier, when David first brought out the horse, and later, while she was still trying unsuccessfully to get up onto Henry's back, but he had disappeared into the barns and she had forgotten he was anywhere around until he opened the bottom half of a partially opened stall door and stepped from the shadows of the barn.

Hank looked at her appraisingly. Leslie knew what he was seeing: battered tennis shoes, clinging sweat-stained clothes, a flushed face, and limp hair straggling over a wilted collar. He tipped his hat to her, a symbolic gesture more than an actual lifting of it, just a thumb and forefinger touched to the brim, then he turned to David.

"If you're going to make your wife western, you'd better outfit her. Start with a hat, Doc," he said, leading Henry toward the barn. "You know better than to bring her out in this sun without one. She ain't made of leather like we are."

Leslie stared silently at Hank's retreating figure. She didn't know him well enough to understand completely what had just happened. Maybe he always talked to David like that. But for just a moment she thought she had read acceptance in his eyes, his actions, and his words.

"Son-of-a-gun," David said in soft surprise. He turned to Leslie, and it was as if he were seeing her flushed features and limp form for the first time. His mouth compressed in a thin line as he studied her. "Hank's right." He draped his arm over her shoulder and turned her toward the house.

His actions were so different from his easy-going attitude of most of the day that Leslie went with him silently. He led her into the house through the French doors of the breakfast room and pulled out a chair for her, half guiding, half pushing her into it. Then, tossing his hat onto the table, he disappeared into the kitchen.

Leslie sank into the chair, lifting her hair from her neck, closing her eyes, and reveling in the cool comfort of air conditioning. She heard noises from the kitchen and then the slight scrape of a boot heel across the polished hardwood floor. She opened her eyes to see David holding out a glass toward her.

"Thanks," she murmured. Still holding her hair off her neck with one hand, she took the glass and drank gratefully of the cool, sweet well water. She looked up at David, smiling her appreciation, and found him still frowning.

"How do you feel?" he asked.

"Feel?" Puzzled, she tried to read the reason behind his frown. "Fine." That wasn't quite true; she knew it the moment she spoke. And from the look David continued to give her, he knew it, too. But for the first time, Leslie realized that he wasn't in much better condition than she was. She gave a little laugh and added ruefully, "At least as fine as anyone can feel when you're hot, sweaty, dirty, and tired."

She watched his mouth slant in the beginning of a smile.

"I shouldn't have kept you out so long. I forgot that you're not used to this heat."

So that was what was bothering him. "You call this heat?" she asked lightly. It was. Oppressive. Sweltering. Draining. But she didn't have to admit it. "You obviously have never spent the month of August in a large city."

"No." He gave a mock shudder. "And I don't intend to."

Leslie sighed and released her damp hair, letting it fall in disarray over her shoulders. "Appearances to the contrary, I won't melt," she said reassuringly. "I'm made of stronger stuff than that. There isn't anything wrong with me that a long, cool shower won't cure."

She wasn't sure he was totally convinced, but he laughed, took her hand when she held it out to him, tugging her from the chair and held it, she thought once again, just a little longer than absolutely necessary— long enough for her body to begin remembering its trembling response to his closeness a few minutes before.

"Shower?" she reminded him.

Slowly he released her hand. "Shower. Yeah. I'm a little rank myself."

Leslie kept her smile fixed firmly in place. Even *rank*, as he called it, with his blue shirt molded to his shoulders and torso, his dark hair damp and curling against his face, David was a damn sight more appealing than any other man she'd ever met. And that was something she hadn't expected, something she hadn't even let herself think about let alone hope for, something that, after this afternoon, she wasn't at all sure she was prepared to cope with.

"Shower," she said again, inanely, easing past him, toward the doorway.

"Leslie." He caught her by the arm, stopping her.

He was serious again, she noted, quietly, intently serious. She wondered what had prompted this mood change.

"Don't push yourself too hard," he told her. "No one expects you to know everything, do everything, *be* everything."

She felt her smile softening, becoming a real one, at his words, at his concern, at his touch. "I won't," she promised.

Upstairs, a cool shower sluiced away everything but her tiredness. Leslie shampooed and dried her hair. Then, wrapped in her short comfortable bathrobe, she wandered into the bedroom, opened the closet doors, and sat on the edge of the bed while she tried to decide what to wear for the rest of the day. Another pair of jeans? Slacks? A dress? The decision seemed so hard as she fought off the exhaustion that for the past several weeks had been so much a part of her life.

She ought to call Madge, she admitted, and reassure her that she hadn't traveled to the wilds of Oklahoma to fall into the clutches of a modern-day Bluebeard. And she ought to call Mike. No matter how valid the reasons, no matter how much Mike had said he didn't mind, she knew the boy had to be concerned about being brought halfway across the country and then thrust into the hands of strangers. Maybe later, after dinner, she and David could call and talk with both of the children.

She tried fighting the yawn that claimed her and then gave in to it, leaning back against the cool, smooth bedspread. She opened one eye and stared at the closet. Dinner, she thought, still undecided about what to wear. Dinner and a long evening with David. Would he kiss her again? Not the fleeting touch of his lips on her forehead that she barely remembered from the night before, but a real kiss? And tonight, when they walked upstairs together, would he lead her into his room instead of stopping at hers?

"Dumb, Leslie," she muttered as she dragged a pillow from beneath the spread and curled around it. This wasn't a first date between two people who had never met before. They were married. She had no reason for saying no to anything he wanted to do. For the first time since agreeing to this marriage, that thought held no fear for her. She chuckled sleepily and hugged the pillow tighter, remembering their afternoon. She didn't want an excuse to say no.

Whatever happened that night, there was one thing she could be sure of, she thought as the effort of holding one eye open became more than she was capable of and she let her eyelid drift down. Tonight, she assured herself, she would not fall asleep on the couch and leave him to spend the evening alone.

David leaned against the doorjamb and studied the sleeping woman. It was his own damned fault, he admitted, but that didn't ease the frustration he felt as he watched her embracing her pillow. She'd been exhausted the day before; the few hours sleep she'd gotten couldn't have done much to allay that. He'd gotten her up before dawn, dragged her all over the ranch, bent her ear with endless talk, and then compounded everything by wearing her out with a needless riding lesson in the afternoon sun.

Her legs were long, surprisingly long for someone of her tiny stature. Revealed now by the short robe that had ridden up on her thighs, they were bent at the knees as she curled around the pillow, pale against the dark green bedspread. As pale as her face had been that morning.

Swearing under his breath, he walked quietly to the bed and knelt beside her. It wasn't just a flush that stained her cheeks; she'd gotten a generous dose of sunburn. He touched his fingers to her wrist as it rested on the pillow. Her skin was cool, not clammy, and her pulse seemed normal. At least her sleep was a healthy one, not one brought on by the heat exhaustion it had taken Hank's not-so-subtle warning to remind him of.

David let his fingers linger on the velvet softness of her wrist. Hank had been right to warn him. And Hank had been right about something else. Leslie wasn't made of leather.

He drew his hand away. And he wasn't made of steel. That riding lesson had been a damned fool thing to do for more than one reason. She had been so animated all day, so full of questions, so eager to learn, so quick to laugh. She'd been like a kid on the first day of school, or someone on the first day of a challenging new job. He'd wanted to make her aware of him, not as a teacher, and not, for God's sake, as an employer, but as a man. What he'd succeeded in doing was making himself painfully aware of her own soft, pliant body. What he'd had to fight to keep from doing was pulling her off Henry and dragging her into the barn for a fierce, uncivilized coupling that, except for his own physical relief, wouldn't have been satisfying for either of them.

He laughed silently and mirthlessly. Something else he had succeeded in doing was shooting all his hopes for the rest of the evening straight to hell.

He could wake her up. He considered that. She needed food. He shook his head and rose to his feet. That was a rationalization, not to deal in rationalizations. A wry smile twisted his mouth as he looked down at her. Asleep, she seemed even more vulnerable, even younger than he knew her to be, and asleep—maybe even awake, he amended—she had no idea of what she was putting him through.

No. He wouldn't wake her. There were logical progressions, and then there were . . . logical progressions. What she needed now was sleep, not some half-starved man doing his damnedest to lure her into his bed.

Leslie awoke to shadows and the serenade of a full orchestra of crickets. Someone—David, she thought groggily, it had to have been David, there was no one else in the house—had placed a light cover over her and had opened the drapes and patio doors to admit the moonlight and soothing night breeze. She tossed back the cover, forced herself from the bed, and walked to the patio door. A quick glance down at the house and then to her left, at the deck that ran past David's room, revealed only moonwashed darkness.

She leaned against the door facing and with one hand massaged the nagging tension in her neck and shoulder. No, at least she hadn't fallen asleep on the couch, she wryly noted to herself.

What had David thought? Should she go to him? Did he want her? Leslie laughed bitterly. David wanted a woman. Needed a woman. That much they had discussed openly and, she'd thought at the time, candidly. He had married her. Did she need more answer than that?

She thought of the peach satin nightgown and robe hanging in her closet. What she ought to do was put it on and walk the few feet down the hall to David's room. This wasn't some one-night stand, for God's sake; it was the second night of her marriage to a man she liked, respected, and, at least a few hours ago, had wanted with a need that shook her with its intensity.

But she didn't move toward the closet. Couldn't move toward the closet. What would David think if she went to him in the middle of the night and invited herself into his bed? She closed her eyes and leaned her head back, listening to the crickets but hearing something far different. Once she'd sworn that names could have no effect on her as long as *she* knew the truth. Names her father had called her even while he was trying to figure out how much his silence about an underage pregnant girl was worth to the Burgesses. Names Michael's parents had called her. Names people she barely knew and who remembered nothing about her but for one shameful truth they whispered when she walked past. Names that even Michael, toward the end, when he'd become so bitter, had thrown at her. Now she knew better. Names hurt. They cut deep, and they never really healed; they just scarred over.

Leslie heard another sound over the chorus of crickets, a distant sound, one she'd heard the night before. She didn't know what made the cry, a bird or an animal, but she recognized the loneliness in it. She knew loneliness intimately. Today she hadn't been lonely. Tonight she ached with it.

David hadn't awakened her. She accepted that, too. If he had, right now she might be lying in his arms, and right now, that was where she wanted to be. Not just for the physical pleasure that she knew instinctively he could give her, but for the sheer luxury of being held protectively, comfortingly, by someone who cared.

Leslie felt tears on her cheeks. That wasn't in the contract. There were a lot of things, she had discovered that day, that were not in that damned contract. She brushed at her cheeks and squared her shoulders. If David Nichols wanted her in his bed, she would go, willingly, but not tonight, and not without an invitation. It was up to him.

Chapter

5

LESLIE RELAXED MORE deeply into the soft webbing of
the poolside lounger and listened to the soft splashing
noises David made as he swam laps the length of the
pool. Gracefully. The way he did everything. With a
steady surety.

She closed her eyes and let the residual heat of the
day and the beauty of her surroundings drain the last of
her tension from her. She was tired, but for the first time
in longer than she cared to remember, it was a pleasant
tiredness, a healthy one.

David had not awakened her before dawn that morning, and when he did wake her, it was with freshly
brewed coffee and easy conversation while she drank

her mandatory two cups and eased into the morning, a luxury she had always enjoyed but seldom been able to have. There had been no recriminations for the night before, no mention of it until Leslie had tried to apologize and David had refused to hear it.

They prepared breakfast together and shared the cleanup, laughing as they bumped into each other in a kitchen designed to be efficient for only one cook. After breakfast David again helped her into the jeep and took her for another tour of the ranch, this time to parts she hadn't seen the day before: cultivated stands of commercial pine timber and seemingly untouched woodlands where signs of wildlife, if not the wildlife itself, were everywhere; lush hay meadows approaching time for their second cutting of the year; pastures where David's own mixture of crossbred cattle and their large, healthy calves grazed contentedly; all enveloped by the protective circle of mountains, and all overshadowed by or opening onto vistas of such wild and untamed beauty that several times Leslie asked David to stop the jeep so that she could simply look, and listen, and *feel*.

Although the morning was laced with Leslie's new awareness of David—an awareness she now realized was rooted in the same uneasiness she had felt for the last few days—the time passed easily and companionably.

At noon, with the sun hanging heavily in the sky and the heat promising to become oppressive, David brought her back to the dim coolness of the house, and after lunch he excused himself to confer with Hank. Leslie had expected he might do that; David had never seemed the type who could completely ignore his responsibilities, and since returning to the house, he had become increasingly preoccupied. But knowing that David had other responsibilities didn't help Leslie as she prowled through his huge house, alone again, trying to find a room, or at least a portion of one, where she could feel comfortable.

Dismayed at her reaction to what was the most beautiful house she'd ever been in, to what was now her home, Leslie randomly picked a book from the unfamiliar titles and, feeling like an intruder, curled onto a corner of the rust-colored sofa in the library. The ranch might belong to David, but the house had been Elaine's. Leslie knew that with a certainty. The woman's presence was all around her, from the studied casual elegance of the furnishings, to the exquisite cut-glass sculpture on the end table, to the books on the shelves. Any doubts she might have had faded when she remembered David's study: warm, welcoming, cheerfully cluttered. David might—probably did—appreciate the beauty of the rest of the house, but he had made that room uniquely his. And she knew—tucking her feet up under her on the couch, defiantly—that if she was going to survive, she would have to find the nerve to make a room, a place in this house, that was uniquely her own.

It seemed like hours before David returned, but it couldn't have been more than one, Leslie knew, if that long.

"Is everything all right?" Leslie asked, gratefully closing the dry and almost incomprehensible philosophy book she'd been trying to read.

"Oh, yes." David lounged in the library doorway, the sleek lines of his body outlined by the light streaming in from behind him. "At least, according to Hank, things are running more smoothly than when I pop in on them at all hours of the day and night, asking questions and interfering with their work." The corners of David's lips curved upward in a smile, but he didn't move toward her. "And also, according to Hank, I've got better things to do than trying to tell him how to do a job he's been doing for more than forty years."

Leslie felt the flush starting at her toes and working

upward. She knew what *things* Hank was talking about, but having a stranger speculate on what she and David were doing or not doing was more than she could cope with.

"So?" he asked, his smile fading. "What shall we do? It's too hot to take you back outside. How about a game of pool? Do you play chess? Poker?"

"David . . ." She shook her head slowly, wanting to open up to him, to tell him how she felt, but no more able to build on Hank's sexual innuendo than David had seemed to be able to do. A rueful smile was all she could manage.

They played a game of pool on the antique, standard-size table in its own specially decorated alcove of the huge den. Showing her how to hold the cue stick, David moved with grim determination as he explained what seemed to be simple rules and then the not-so-simple techniques of "spin" and "English" and "bank shots."

Not until far into the game, when Leslie looked over her shoulder as David was once again showing her how to hold the cue and caught the tortured expression in his eyes before he had a chance to mask it, did she realize why he was acting so unnaturally stiff. Her breath caught in her throat, but she turned back toward the table, hiding her knowledge behind a quip about the devious mentality that had invented the game. *David wanted her.* As much as she wanted him. But for some reason he was not acting on that desire. For some reason he did not even want her to know about it.

Leslie missed the shot. David took control of the table and quickly cleared it. Then, without asking if she wanted to play another game, he returned the cue sticks to their fitted rack.

Leslie was slightly more knowledgeable about a chess board than a pool table, but she was more interested in David than any game, attempting to joke with him, making comments about their morning, drawing him out. He won that game, too, although not quite so decisively, but by the end of it, he was acting almost naturally, almost like the David she'd already come to rely upon.

"How about a game of poker?" he asked as he repositioned the chess pieces.

Almost natural, Leslie realized. *Almost* like himself. But not quite.

She leaned back in her chair and looked up at him quizzically from beneath one cocked eyebrow. "Do you think that's fair? I know you've beaten me twice, but..."

His expression tightened until Leslie giggled at his look of dismay, a surprisingly young sound which surprised even her and destroyed her attempt at teasing.

"Better me for a teacher than Hank Baker," David said. He took a large dish of roasted peanuts from a nearby table, shelled one, and ate it, then dumped the remainder on the table, dividing them and pushing half toward Leslie. "We'll use these for chips," he explained, responding to her quizzical glance. "Hank and Mabel come over to the house for an occasional friendly game, but the problem in waiting for Hank to teach you is that he has a tendency to change the rules."

He looked across at her as he began shuffling a deck of cards. "It's okay, isn't it?" he asked, smiling questioningly, but smiling, for the first time since they'd left the library.

She grinned back at him. She knew she ought to say something, but his assumption that he was going to introduce her to yet another strange activity, as gently and carefully presented as it might be, kept her silent.

He finished shuffling the cards and placed them on the table in front of her, resting his hand on top of them. "The rules are pretty simple."

For a moment she fought the impulse, then placed

her hand on his, feeling his small start of surprise. This much she had to tell him. "David, I know the rules."

Forty-five minutes later, all of the peanuts, or at least what was left of them, were on her side of the table, and she'd watched David progress through a variety of moods, from patient determination, to surprise, to mock outrage, then to genuine enjoyment.

"Do you think that's fair?" he teased gently, laughing as he reached for one of the few intact peanuts.

She slapped his hand playfully. "How am I going to know how much I won if you keep eating them?"

"Where did you learn to play poker like that?"

Leslie's laughter died. Maybe she had something to thank her father for after all. He had taught her two things in her life: how to play poker and how little he cared for her or for anyone else. "From my father," she said tightly, "who, the last I heard, was a dealer in Atlantic City."

Leslie had told David a few things about her father—how he had flitted in and out of her life and her mother's, how he had shown up at the last minute when her mother was dying, and had seemed to assume the responsibility thrust upon him, how he had later tried to force Leslie to have an abortion, how he had tried to blackmail Michael and his family. Now she wished she had said nothing; David was too sensitive to the unwanted mood her memories evoked.

"So," she asked, gathering peanuts and hulls and dumping them in the bowl. She gave him a too bright smile, to which he didn't respond. "What next?"

What next? Leslie thought again as she listened to the sounds of David pulling himself from the pool. It was a question that had worried her more than once that afternoon as she watched David work at nonchalance, at casual friendliness, seeming more like a tour guide or a social director than the virile, healthy man she knew him to be—or thought him to be?—No, what she *knew* him to be, she decided firmly.

She didn't have to open her eyes to know he was coming toward her. She was almost painfully aware of him, had been all afternoon as he filled their time with nonstrenuous, meaningless activities, treating her, whether he realized it or not, as if she were some fragile child that had to be protected from all but the most pampered of conditions. He hadn't even suggested a swim until after the sun had dropped low enough in the sky and the pool was shaded by the bulk of the house.

Well, she wasn't going to break, had never broken, in fact, but short of repeating what she'd told him the day before and which he obviously hadn't believed, she knew of no way to convince him. And in spite of David's efforts, or maybe because of them, the afternoon had taken a toll on her as she struggled to hide the growing pull she felt between the two of them, a pull so strong it should have been physical, should have been visible, a cord binding them and crackling with the current that a simple look or inadvertent touch could spark to life. How hard she had tried to hide the desire, to follow David's lead, to tease him into a laughter they both could share. What effort it had taken to ignore all the signals her body was telegraphing to her mind just in case she'd misread the look in his eyes and the occasional tense lapses in their conversation.

He was standing beside her now—she didn't have to open her eyes to know that, either. She *felt* him there, along all her nerve endings, his presence so real that he might as well have been touching her. Eyes still closed, she clamped down on her thoughts and searched for something to say, something light, casual, and in keeping with all that had been said before.

At the first drop of icy water on her heated flesh, her

eyes flew open and she jerked upright in the lounger. "What—"

David leaned over her, his hand still dripping pool water along her arm. "You weren't asleep."

His dark eyes were softened with lazy humor and something else, an expression that was gone so quickly that Leslie couldn't define it, couldn't even be sure she hadn't imagined it. But she wasn't imagining what the sight of him clad in nothing but the moderately cut black bathing suit was doing to her senses. That was why she'd retreated to the lounger and closed her eyes in the first place. He was all-over tan, a deep bronze undershot with that marvelous copper hue that no cosmetic manufacturer has ever been able to duplicate— all-over lean muscle and strength, and now, with drops of water still clinging to his smooth chest and the fine line of black hair tracking its way down his taut abdomen and flat belly, so close, she thought, that with almost no effort she could move her hand from where it rested on the arm of the lounger to rest instead against the supple texture of his thigh. She clasped her fingers firmly around the armrest.

"Scoot over," he said.

Without thinking, Leslie did so. He dropped onto the lounger, and Leslie felt his thigh, still wet, slightly abrasive from the fine dusting of dark hair along it, slide against her own heated flesh as he sat down beside her.

"Don't get too comfortable, sleepyhead," he warned gently, placing his hand over hers on the armrest. "It's time to start thinking about dinner."

Leslie searched for censure in his words, censure of her having fallen asleep two nights in a row, but could find none. A heat far different from sunstroke or the ever-present humidity raced through her—heat from their two points of contact, his thigh against hers, his hand on hers. But he didn't seem aware of any of it.

She leaned back against the lounger and grinned

cheekily at him. "Food?" she asked. "Here I am, sun-
burned, saddle sore, and weary from a hard day on the
ranch, and the man wants to think about food?"

The flip comment drew no response from him, and
Leslie's grin faded as she realized there was no need for
it. He wasn't watching her face; he was studying their
hands. With one finger he traced a pattern along hers,
down, across, and back over the wide engraved band he
had placed there two days before.

"Leslie." David's voice seemed to come from somewhere deep inside him. "This isn't working."

Her breath caught, suspended somewhere in limbo
with her heartbeat, and her voice lodged in her throat.
Nothing had been as simple as either of them had
planned, nothing had gone the way she'd thought it
would, but was David telling her he wanted out of their
arrangement? No, she decided quickly. David was an
honorable man, she knew that much without questioning it. He would abide by their agreement. But knowing
he'd changed his mind, could she remain where she
wasn't wanted?

She found her breath and her voice, and forced them
out in a thready imitation of what was normal. "What
do you mean?"

"I mean—" Still he didn't look at her, just continued
stroking her hand, almost as though he didn't even realize he was doing it. "I mean, I thought I'd be able to
keep my hands off you."

Leslie felt muscles she hadn't realized she'd tensed
relax and her heartbeat resumed at a rate about half its
normal speed, but she kept her voice low and even.
"Why ever would you want to do a thing like that?"

He turned to face her, smiling bleakly. "Because after
what you've been through, you need a chance to rest
and regroup. Because, in spite of all we thought, you
really don't know me." He looked away from her, toward the trees beyond the flagstone deck. "Because I

don't want you doing anything because you feel you have to."

"David . . ." Leslie shook her head in slow denial. She lifted her free hand and rested it against his cheek, directing his gaze back to her, and spoke softly. "Two nights ago, I might have felt that way, at first. But that feeling wouldn't have lasted. It hasn't lasted."

His eyes were a warm satin brown as he gazed down at her, so dark, so deep, she knew she would never be able to understand all the secrets they held, but the one she did understand was at last revealed to her in the expression she had glimpsed throughout the afternoon. This time he didn't attempt to hide it; this time she knew it wasn't her imagination.

"I *am* your wife," she reminded him gently.

A spasm of what could have been pain passed across his beautiful features. After long seconds, he slid his hand from hers, around her and lifted her to him.

"I want you," he murmured into the mass of her hair as he held her motionless against his chest. "I never thought I would want anyone as much as I want you."

"And I want you," she whispered shakily. It was the hardest thing she'd ever had to say, not because it wasn't true—it was—but because years of repressing her needs, her desires, her emotions, had made it so.

He tightened his arms around her and found her mouth in a kiss so gently persuasive it brought tears to her eyes. She felt a tremor run through him and recognized the cause of it—need, raw, elemental, as great as her own. She lifted her hands to his back, felt the play of muscles beneath her touch, the strength, the power now held tightly in check, and parted her lips, inviting him silently to deepen the kiss.

She felt the velvet harshness of his tongue along her inner lips, heard him groan, then was overwhelmed by his need, no longer checked, as he crushed her to him and swept her with him into a maelstrom of longing so intense she ached from it. She felt his tongue, finding the hidden sweetness of her mouth and imitating the deeper intimacies yet to come, his hands, not grasping as she would have thought had she been able to think, but persuasive in their possession as they moved over her, sliding from the skimpy fabric of the bathing suit to her overheated flesh which now moved restlessly beneath his touch.

He moved his hand between them, upward, to cup a breast she'd always thought too small, too insignificant to give much pleasure, let alone receive much, and she felt that breast swell, straining against his hand, tugging at a pulse deep within her and impatient for more than the brush of his thumb against the fabric that covered it.

She heard a click, and the back of the lounger lowered, taking her and David with it, until she lay beneath the length of him. She felt his mouth on her throat, moving downward, his hands on the straps of her suit, sliding them away, the kiss of the now cool breeze on her bare breasts before David covered one with his mouth, the other with his hand.

Leslie heard a moan and realized dimly that it had been torn from her, vaguely sensing she had shifted beneath him so that she now held the heat of his arousal cradled against her. She reached for him, wanting to return the pleasure he was giving her yet unsure of how to do it, and unable to reach anything but the richness of his hair, the muscles of his shoulders and the arms now straining as he held his weight from her.

David sighed and abruptly sagged against her, and she held him, feeling the tension that still gripped him.

"What am I doing?" he asked.

He lifted his head, and she saw that his eyes were hooded, as dazed as her own must be. Incapable of speech, she remained silent, waiting, not understanding why he'd stopped.

He rolled away from her and sat on the edge of the

lounger, breathing deeply, gathering his composure,
but, as she recognized gratefully, not withdrawing from
her in any way but touch.

"This place is private," he said ruefully, turning toward her and slowly pulling her suit up to cover her,
"but not this private."

He let his hand linger on the slope of her breast,
then, bending toward her, touched her lips with a kiss
that was chaste in comparison to what they'd just experienced. His eyes held hers. "Will you go inside with
me, Leslie?"

Leslie closed her eyes and swallowed once, but that
didn't clear the constriction in her throat. Even now, he
was giving her another chance to say no. It would have
been so much easier if he'd simply taken her by the
hand and led her across the flagstones surrounding the
pool and up the wooden stairs that led to the second-
story deck and his bedroom. But he was making the
choice hers. There would be no way she could ever
claim that she was being carried away by the heat of a
passion that wasn't hers, that he had overpowered her,
coerced her, or pressured her into anything she didn't
want. She opened her eyes, surprised and torn by the
path her thoughts had taken. She did want this; why
should she deny it? Why should she want to deny it?
Still, her smile was hesitant as she nodded, lifted her
hand and placed it in his.

Inside the dim coolness of David's bedroom, Leslie's
courage deserted her. She'd been there only once before, the day after she arrived, the day David had given
her a brief tour of the house and ranch buildings. She'd
remembered it all, the massive stone fireplace flanked
on each side by matching French doors that led out to a
private area of the wrap-around deck; the sitting alcove;
the doors to the oversized bathroom and the spacious
closets. But now all that was in focus was the queen-
sized bed with its tailored spread and the subtle traces of

Elaine's personality that she had found in the rest of the house.

"Leslie." David spoke slowly and hesitantly as he cupped her face in his hands and looked deep into her eyes. "It's been a long time for me. I . . ."

All thoughts of Elaine faded as Leslie realized that David was concerned not about his image, not even, really, about his performance, but about her. It was the tentative way he held her that told her. She found a smile for him and reached her hands to his arms.

"Don't worry about me," she told him softly. "Every time doesn't have to be—" She searched for a subtle word but could find none. "Every time doesn't have to be cataclysmic. Sometimes just the caring—and the sharing—is enough."

He traced his fingers along her cheek. "You give so much," he said raggedly. "I don't think even you realize how much. And I think it's been a hell of a long time since anyone other than Mike gave anything back to you."

His eyes clouded before he drew her to him. "Don't let me hurt you, Leslie."

Don't let me hurt you because I can't give you anything either. Leslie heard the unspoken words as she went into his arms. "I won't," she promised as she surrendered her mouth to his and he began, once again, to lead her to that state where she was aware of nothing but the two of them.

Her legs failed to support her. She felt the smooth brush of the bedspread beneath her as David guided her toward it and began with infinite patience to lower her bathing suit, following its slow path with his mouth, with his touch, until she was freed from the fabric. With a whisper of material, he freed himself from his own trunks and lowered himself beside her, taking her in his arms for a kiss that probed at her soul and left her breathless and aching.

She felt his arousal, heavy and persistent against her thigh, but he made no move to take her. Instead, he began again with mouth and touch to trace the paths he'd already followed, teaching her areas of her body she had only dreamed could be so responsive, showing her others she had never suspected.

Her body was alive and quivering with sensations too long denied, too long forgotten, and when she felt his lips and the rasp of his tongue at the core of those sensations, Leslie cried out, mingling pleasure, embarrassment, anticipation, and longing in one incomprehensible moan. That couldn't be her breathing she heard, harsh and irregular, but it was. That couldn't be her voice, murmuring, pleading, but it was. And it couldn't be her body, stretched bow-string tight with a miracle beginning somewhere deep inside it, but it was, and Leslie knew that this was something she must share.

She tugged at David and forced her voice to form words. "Please. Not alone. Not alone," she whispered urgently. "I want you with me."

Instantly he was above her, holding her tight. There was a brief fumbling, two unfamiliar bodies reaching for each other, then not only was he above her, around her, surrounding her with his warmth, but within her, filling her.

The shock of his possession stunned her, bringing her a moment of sanity. *What was she doing?* She looked up at him, seeing the need in his eyes and feeling the tremors of her own need. This was her husband, she reminded herself. The memory of Michael flitted through her consciousness. No. Not Michael. Never again Michael. This man, even though he made no claim to love her, was far more caring than Michael had ever been. And that was enough. *More than enough*.

She lifted her hands to clasp his face and bring his mouth to hers. "David," she murmured against his lips. "David."

Then he was moving with her, leading her onward. She had no control, only the nameless longing, the glorious pressure building within her, but she felt the moment his control began to slip. She pressed her fingers into the taut muscles of his buttocks and arched against him, this time urging him. He groaned, either in defeat, or triumph, and his smooth, careful movements became demanding, insistent. Leslie could not begin to match them, to pace them, all she could do was hold onto David as he plunged headlong into ecstasy, taking her with him.

Chapter
6

THE RETURN OF the children, two days early, brought an end to the unexpected and too-brief idyll. Grace Nichols called late Saturday morning, apologetic but firm in her intent to bring Ellie and Mike home.

Leslie had grown accustomed to David's closeness, the touch of his hand on her arm, her shoulder, her waist, but the sight of Mike's sullen expression and Ellie's white face so dismayed her it was some time before she realized he had moved several inches away from her, distant in more than space and betraying none of the intimacy the two of them had been sharing.

"Get the packages out of the car and then take everything up to your rooms," Grace said to the children, then stood silently, her mouth fixed in a grim line until the children were upstairs and out of hearing range.

"They weren't prepared, David," she said. "None of us were, perhaps not even you and Leslie, but they less than anyone. I'm sorry I couldn't give you the time I promised, but I thought it better to bring them home, to the two of you, before the situation got completely out of hand. They both need reassuring, they both need understanding, and they both need a lot of love right now, and, while I've tried, I'm not the one they want it from."

Leslie found that she had unconsciously edged closer to David, but he seemed unaware of her.

"Come on downstairs," he said to his mother, "and tell me what happened."

Puzzled by David's withdrawal from her, and unwilling to face more of the criticism she saw so clearly written in Grace's expression, Leslie hesitated on the top step.

"I'll—" It was a coward's escape, she knew that, but she also knew it was necessary. "I'll go check on the children."

David glanced over his shoulder at her, searching her eyes with his. "Yes," he said. "That might be a good idea. Go ahead. I'll be up in a minute."

Leslie hurried up the stairs, but as she approached the bedroom wing, she slowed her steps, hesitant about how to approach Mike and Ellie. She and David should have spent more time with them before the wedding, should have called them days before when Leslie had first thought of it, should be talking together with them now, but they hadn't, and they weren't. She hadn't intended for her statement to sound like a request for permission, but it had. And maybe David hadn't meant his answer to sound as though he were granting permission, but it had.

The past few days had been so wonderful, Leslie had forgotten that she and David were playing at marriage. No. Not playing. Working very hard at one. With well-

defined boundaries and responsibilities. And her responsibilities included keeping his home as conflict free as
possible and helping his daughter break out of her self-
imposed shell to become the happy, natural child she
had been.

She went to Mike's room first. He had dumped the
contents of various sacks onto his bed but had gotten no
further. He was sitting on the edge of the bed, surrounded by jeans and western shirts, a pair of boots, and
a hat, wearing the same sullen expression he had worn
when she'd picked him up at the police station the day
his best friend had been caught shoplifting.

Leslie cleared a place and sat beside him on the bed,
waiting for him to speak first, knowing from long experience that eventually he would.

And, eventually, he did, although Leslie had begun
to think she was going to have to prompt him. He turned
to her, his eyes full of rebellion, and jutted out his chin.
"Do I have to be a cowboy?"

Leslie glanced at the array of clothing, shrugged, and
shook her head. "No. Not if you don't want to be."

That took some of the anger out of his expression,
and Leslie searched carefully for the words that would
remove the rest of it.

"It would be a new experience for you, something
you might enjoy if you gave it a chance." She picked up
the hat and traced her finger around the straw brim.
"You'll have chores, of course, you've always had
chores, and some of them might be ranch related, but no
one is going to *make* you be a cowboy. In fact," she
said, placing the hat to one side, "I understand that not
everybody *can* be."

A snort was his only comment for a few moments,
then he glanced sideways at her. "Do I have to call him
Dad?"

Leslie wished she'd kept the hat in her hands. With
something to hold, she wouldn't have found it nearly so

hard to keep from touching Mike's cheek, to smooth the hair out of his eyes, to hold him. "No," she said calmly. "But if you ever want to, I think David would be happy for you to call him Dad."

"What *do* I call him?" Mike insisted. "*Sir*? *Doctor Nichols*?"

Leslie fought the grin she felt building, but the corners of her lips curved upward. Mike was having to work now at being belligerent. "An occasional 'yes, sir' or 'no, sir' won't hurt you, Mike, but how about just calling him David?" she suggested.

He grinned back at her sheepishly. "I guess you're right. 'Please pass the butter, Doctor Nichols' would sound kind of silly, wouldn't it?"

"Kind of," she said, smiling at him and fighting the need to hug him.

"Mom?" he asked, suddenly serious, and Leslie knew he had finally gotten to the heart of the problem. "Can we leave?"

A quick no couldn't answer this question; a flip comment couldn't either. "Why would we want to, Mike?" she asked hesitantly. "We just got here. This is a beautiful home, and we have a chance at a wonderful new life."

"I don't mean right now," he said irritably. "I mean, *can* we? If we want to?"

Leslie leaned away from him slightly, studying him as she formed her answer.

"Ellie said we couldn't," he told her. "She said we had to stay here forever. She said that's what marrying somebody and being a mommy meant. Does this mean I can't ever see my grandmother and grandfather again, or Scooter or Jackie, or any of my friends?"

Leslie rubbed her hand across her forehead, raking her fingers through her hair. "Michael James Burgess," she said, sighing, "why do you ask such hard questions?"

Because he's afraid. Because in spite of his air of bravado, he's still a little boy who doesn't understand.

She took a deep breath and turned to him, placing her hands on his shoulders. "About the first part of your question: can we leave? This isn't a prison, Mike. I brought us here because I wanted to come, and if ever there is a time when I really, truly, want to leave, we can. But yes, marrying somebody does mean that you want to live with that person forever, and being a mommy does mean that you love your child and you don't ever want to be separated."

"And my grandmother and grandfather? They wanted me to be with them this summer. They were going to take me to Maine, and deep-sea fishing, and all my things are at their house. Grandmother said you didn't want me to be with them, that you'd try to keep me away from them. That's why you brought me out here, isn't it? So I couldn't go with them?"

Leta had said that? Leta had actually said that to Mike? Would the woman stop at nothing?

Leslie grasped Mike's shoulders. "Yes." When he tried to twist away from her, she held him still. "I wasn't going to tell you this, Mike, and I don't want to tell you now, but you need to know. Your grandparents love you very much, but they didn't want you to come to them just for the summer. They wanted you to live with them."

"That would be neat," he said. "There's plenty of room for us in their house—"

She shook her head, knowing she had to be careful, and knowing she had to make him understand. "Not *us* Mike, *you*. They wanted me to give you to them and never see you again."

Leslie watched the bewilderment in Mike's eyes. "I don't want to separate you from them forever, but I don't want you placed in the position of having to choose between them and me. They're your family, too,

Mike, and you're all they have now that your dad is dead. I just wanted to get us away long enough for them to realize that your loving me doesn't mean you can't love them. I hope that one day they can realize that, and when they do, yes, I'll tell them where we are and you will be able to see them again. But," she added, hearing her words and knowing how they must sound to a twelve-year-old, "that's only one of the reasons we came."

"They don't even know where we are? Then how are you going to know when they change their mind?"

She smiled at him and gave in to the need to touch his cheek. "I'll know. And I want you to write to them. There are a lot of things we can't tell them right now, but you can let them know that you're okay, that you're happy."

"And they can write to me?"

Leslie dropped her hand back to his shoulder. This was something she hadn't quite worked out. Madge had volunteered to remail Mike's letters, but Leslie couldn't even consider subjecting her to the pressure the Burgesses would exert if they knew she was aware of Leslie's address. "Not right away," she told Mike. "But soon, I hope." *As soon as she felt safe enough.*

"So?" she asked when Mike remained silent. "Is anything else bothering you?"

He shook his head. "Only that I met about ten thousand people this week and Ellie kept telling me they were my cousins."

Leslie knew that David was an only child, but she also knew that Grace came from a large family. Mike must be talking about the children of Phil and Ben and a whole clan of Wilcoxes that she had yet to meet. "Second cousins, I think," she told Mike. "How did you get along with them?"

"Okay, I guess," he admitted uncertainly, "but they all kept talking about riding horses and going hunting, and no one knows how to play soccer. But they were okay, I guess. Except for Ellie. She's really weird."

Leslie kept her expression neutral and her voice light. "How so?"

"I mean—she's just a little *kid*, Mom, but she acts worse than old Mrs. Siedman in our building back home. 'May I get you something to drink, Mike? Welcome to the family, Mike.'" he mimicked. "Aren't girls supposed to play with dolls or something?"

"Or something," Leslie told him.

"Well, Ellie doesn't play. Not with anything. Weird."

"Mike." She hated to remind him, but this was something they had talked about many times as they had worked through their grief together, and Mike needed to understand that he and Ellie did have more in common than the roof over their heads. "Do you remember how you felt when your dad died? How you were hurt, and afraid, and even angry?"

Mike hung his head, refusing to look at her, but he nodded.

"Well, Ellie wasn't much older than you were when she lost her mom. And her brother. And was hurt very badly. She's had three operations, and she's just now beginning to walk right. Don't you think she has reasons for being a little bit different? At least for a while?"

"Yeah," he mumbled. "When you put it that way..."

Leslie ruffled his hair and leaned toward him. "I know you think you're too old for this," she told him, "but humor me. I need it." She slid her arms around him and was rewarded by his answering, fierce hug.

Facing Ellie was a little more difficult. Leslie paused outside Ellie's door hoping to hear the comforting tones of David's voice from inside the room, or to see him striding down the hallway toward her. When she accepted that neither of those two things was going to happen, she pushed open the door and stepped inside.

Like Mike, Ellie sat on the edge of the bed, surrounded by packages. Unlike with Mike, Leslie didn't know how to approach her. She pushed aside a package and seated herself beside Ellie. Apparently Grace Nichols thought Ellie ought to be playing, too, Leslie noted, as a large floppy rag doll slid from the sack she moved.

"It's all right to tell me," she said when Ellie remained silent. "It won't be like tattling, and you won't get Mike into any trouble."

Ellie looked up at her but remained silent.

"We're a family now, Ellie, and families talk to each other, and tell each other what's wrong, and help each other get through whatever is bothering them."

A tear quivered on Ellie's lash, broke free and trailed down her cheek. Reflexively, without thinking, Leslie reached for her. Ellie backed away, swiping at her cheeks with both hands. "I don't *ever* cry."

Leslie knew what Mike meant. It was a strangely adult gesture, an awkwardly grown-up tone of voice coming from a tiny little girl. *Oh, darling,* she wanted to say, *you need to cry. Let me hold you while you do. Let me love you while you pour it all out.* If anyone needed to be held, trembling and troubled Ellie Nichols was that person.

Leslie reached instead for the rag doll. "This looks like a nice doll," she offered encouragingly.

"I'm a big girl. I don't need dolls."

"Oh?" Leslie asked. "Well, I don't know for sure, but this looks like a big girl's doll. A friend doll more than a baby doll. I always wanted a doll like this." As Leslie spoke the words, she knew they were true. She had missed so much, had been catapulted into maturity too fast. Ellie'd had so much taken from her already, and with a sense of fierce protectiveness, Leslie determined that Ellie wouldn't lose her childhood, too.

She held the doll to her in a loose embrace, showing Ellie that it wasn't shameful or degrading to do so, and spoke in a careful, thoughtful way. "Even big girls need love, Ellie. I know I do. There's nothing wrong with it; it's the way we are. We all need to know we're loved, and we all need to be able to give love."

"Are you going away?" Ellie asked abruptly. "Mike said you were. He said he was going to make you take him back to New Jersey."

"Oh, honey." Leslie dropped the doll and reached for Ellie, not knowing whether her embrace would be welcomed or not, but knowing that Ellie needed to be held. As she gathered the girl into her arms she saw David standing just inside the doorway. She didn't know how long he'd been there or how much he'd heard, but as their eyes met over Ellie's head, his were suspiciously bright.

"No, Ellie," he said walking to the bed, his eyes still holding Leslie's, "Leslie isn't going away. I promise you that."

Leslie surrendered Ellie to his arms and watched with a tight throat and blurred vision while the big girl who never cried sobbed disconsolately against her father's chest.

They made it through the day. Later, Leslie couldn't find any other way to describe the remainder of that afternoon and evening. She had no idea what David had said to Ellie, or later to Mike, after she slipped from the room to seek out his mother.

Hesitantly, she thanked Grace Nichols for her thoughtfulness in providing the cake for them, for the presents, and for caring for the children, apologizing for the inconvenience she'd been put through.

Instead of the criticism she half expected, the woman stopped on the front steps and turned to her, smiling. "No apologies are necessary, Leslie. Underneath all his swagger, Mike is a basically a good boy. You've done a fine job raising him." Grace's smile faded. "But I'm afraid all of you are going to have some problems adjusting to a new family." She reached for Leslie's hand and clasped it loosely. "Call me if I can help."

Then, once again smiling, she stepped into her car and drove away, leaving Leslie standing on the step feeling foolish and confused.

Whatever David had said to the children had its effect on them. They were almost normal in behavior the rest of the afternoon, slipping only occasionally. It was as if a truce had been declared, fragile and tentative, but nonetheless working, between Ellie and Mike, between Mike and David, and even, although she had no idea of the reason for it, between David and herself.

After dinner, after the children had gone to bed, Leslie thought that she and David might talk, might recapture some of the closeness they'd shared. They did talk—about the children, about the day; and she even initiated a conversation about his mother's kindness—and he seemed closer than he had in hours, but the magic of the past few days was gone.

Later, he walked with her up the stairs. She'd shared his bed for the last two nights—and two days—but they'd never gotten around to moving her things from her room to his, had never even discussed whether they would. Now, with this new strangeness between them, she was again unsure of herself. At the door to her room, she hesitated.

"I need you," he said.

Surprised by the intensity in his voice, she looked up at him, trying to read the reason for it in his eyes. *And I need you,* she thought, echoing that intensity. *Probably not for the same reasons, but more than I thought I would ever need another person. How did we get to this point, David? And what do I do now?* There were no answers, not for any of her questions. Later, perhaps, she would find some. Now there was only one thing she could do, only one thing she wanted to do. She smiled at him and continued walking down the hall, toward his room.

While Leslie prepared for bed, David opened one of the French doors and stood looking out over the night. He was still standing there when, for the first time dressed in the exquisite peach satin, she walked to him and slid her arm around his waist. He hugged her close to his side, then turned her in his arms and covered her mouth with a kiss that filled her with tender yearning although it was almost completely without passion.

"Go on to bed," he told her. "I'll be there in a minute."

Leslie slid between the sheets and lay watching him for several minutes before he turned from the window and walked to the bed. When he slid in beside her, he gathered her close to him, holding her with one arm under her shoulders, but instead of beginning the long, slow seduction of her senses she'd expected from his words, he smoothed the hair away from her forehead and cheek and kissed her once again. "Good night, Leslie."

She looked at him in confusion, but he'd already dropped his head to the pillow and closed his eyes. Only the tension she sensed gripping him and the stroking of his hand against her arm told her that he was still awake. Gradually, she felt the tension ebbing from him and the stroking slow, then stop.

Long after David's even breathing told her that he was sleeping, Leslie lay awake. *Big girls don't cry.* That was what Ellie had tried to insist. That was what Leslie had always tried to believe. But they did. At last she recognized why Ellie's actions had seemed so familiar. Leslie fought back tears the same way, swiping at them with her hands, holding them in check, denying their right to fall.

She looked toward David, saw his chest rising and falling rhythmically in the moonlight, saw the harsh set of his features, unrelaxed even in sleep, felt a pain in him much deeper than anything she had expected. *And what about big boys?* she asked silently. *Can't they cry either?* But again, she found no answers.

She discovered that she was uncomfortable in his embrace. Her neck was bent at an odd angle, her elbow trapped between them, squeezed against her breast. She shifted slightly, intending to move away, but his arm trapped her. She smiled into the night, shaking her head imperceptibly. No. She wouldn't move away from him. Too often she had longed to be held just this way.

She turned on her side, toward him. Her elbow was a problem, but after a moment's study, she bent her arm and slid her hand under his shoulder as she tucked her head more comfortably against him. Now her other arm seemed awkward and out of place. With only a moment's hesitation, she lifted it and placed her hand on David's chest, above his heart. He stirred once in his sleep, drawing her even closer. Her senses were filled with him, with the texture of his skin, the strength of his arms, the rhythm of his breath and heartbeat, the lingering aroma of soap mingled with his own masculine scent. She breathed deeply, then matched her breathing with his. In minutes, long before she thought it possible, sleep carried her into peaceful oblivion.

Chapter

7

EVEN BIG GIRLS need love. David looked at the ledgers spread out on his desk but saw instead an image he'd seen too many times over the past month—that of Leslie's face as she held his daughter and repeated those words endlessly in his memory.

Leslie needed love, too. Even though she never asked for it, even though she denied that need. He saw it in the way she responded to the slightest kindness, the slightest warmth, drinking in affection the way this poor, parched mountain soil drank in water in August. And in the way she gave love. Naturally, without her being aware of it, it poured from her—to Ellie, to Mike, to anyone who showed the slightest willingness to accept it—even to him.

Had he cheated her? Had he done her more harm

than good by bringing her here? God knew she had been good for him, more than living up to the naive expectations he'd had for their marriage. For the first time in years, his home was a home, its stark lines softened imperceptibly by her presence, its sterile loneliness permeated by the light floral perfume she wore, by her ready, gentle laughter.

Things weren't perfect; even he hadn't been foolish enough to expect perfection. He still had to face Mike's inevitable jealousy, and there were still outbursts between Mike and Ellie, but at least Ellie had opened up enough to let some of her feelings show. Leslie had done that for her. In the space of a few days, she'd accomplished more than David had in years.

Big girls need love, too. He heard her words again and gave up on his ledgers. If he'd been a few minutes later that afternoon, he would never have heard her speak those words and wouldn't now be hearing them, wouldn't hear them at night when he turned to her and she came into his arms, inhibitions finally gone, responding to him with a passion that never ceased to surprise him or delight him, wouldn't hear them whenever the children or someone else was present and he longed to touch her or give her some small sign of affection.

Had he cheated her? he wondered again. He'd kept his promises to her. Mike's adoption was well underway. The Burgesses hadn't found her. In the month since their marriage, Leslie had regained her normal weight, her eyes had lost that haunted, shadowed look, and long hours in the sun had tanned her pale complexion to a warm golden glow. But was that really enough for her? He knew it wasn't. Leslie deserved someone to love; she deserved someone who could return her love. Well, he'd fight like hell to keep her—suddenly David sat up straight in his chair, its unoiled spring squeaking in protest, as he realized where his thoughts had taken him. Why had he thought that? He didn't know. And after a minute he realized he didn't have to understand *why* to know that it was true—as true as something else he didn't understand: that he couldn't be the one to return her love.

Leslie's words weren't the only thing that haunted him while he held her. Sometimes the memory of Elaine forced its way into his thoughts. At first he'd tried to push her memory away, not knowing which shocked him most—feeling guilty about holding another woman while thinking about Elaine, or feeling disloyal to Leslie as his thoughts returned to Elaine—but he'd quickly realized how foolish either of those feelings was. Elaine had been part of his life for fifteen years, ever since he had first seen her in an undergraduate chemistry class, and Leslie—at least for the next six years or until the Burgesses dropped their insane plan to take Mike from her—Leslie was part of his future.

He would always love Elaine, but she was gone, irretrievably lost to him on a wooded mountaintop in the wreckage of the small blue and white Cessna he'd bought for her and had taught her to fly; but he knew he couldn't turn the remainder of his life into a shrine for lost love. Elaine herself would have been the first to ridicule him if he even tried.

So why, then, did he still feel so tied to her? Guilt? *No.* He'd been over that time after time in his mind. He was not responsible for her death or Tommy's. Hindsight was damning. There were always so many things, viewed from the distance of time, that could have altered the past. He wouldn't—couldn't—dwell on the if onlys and the could have beens, not if he wanted to keep his sanity.

"It's hotter than nine kinds of hell out there," Hank said as he let himself into the air-conditioned office and leaned back against the door, wiping a limp, long-sleeved arm across his forehead. At David's noncommital reply, he glanced at the ledgers. "'Bout to figure out if we're gonna get paid this month, boss?"

In spite of the gloomy turn his thoughts had taken, David found himself smiling. For as long as he could remember, Hank had found at least one occasion a year to ask that question. It was a tradition that had its roots in something that took place long before David was born, back when David's father and Hank might have had reason to worry about payroll, but there was no evidence now of worry in Hank's voice as he went through the familiar ritual.

"I think we'll manage," David said dryly. "How's the hay coming?"

"We've got a little problem with that," Hank said, walking to the refrigerator and taking out a long-necked bottle of beer. "Thought I'd better check with you."

David leaned back in his chair. Hank never brought him little problems, so this had to be either major or involving a sensitive area. "What's the matter, Hank? Aren't we going to have enough feed for the winter?"

Hank snorted and took a long pull from his beer. "Not unless it starts snowing tomorrow and doesn't stop until next June. That's the problem. The storage barns are full and we still have trucks coming in." He took another drink and studied David quietly. "I figured we could use that fancy horse barn of yours, and maybe part of the hangar. Unless you've got some other idea."

Not major, David thought, but definitely sensitive. Still, Hank was offering him the only logical solution to the problem and leaving the decision up to him. And not *his* fancy horse barn, either, but Elaine's—empty since he'd sold her horses. And a hangar that now housed only one dusty, unused single-engine plane instead of the two well-maintained and often used airplanes it had been designed for.

"The hay has to go somewhere. There's no point in cutting it and baling it if we're going to leave it out in the weather to ruin." David pushed himself up from his chair. "Use what you need."

Hank nodded and waved his bottle in the general direction of the house. "You've got a crowd gathering."

"Already?" David glanced at his watch and frowned when he saw the time.

"Yeah. Already. Mabel went over about two to help Leslie get set up, and I saw your mom's car come through a little after that. There's about six cars up there now, and it don't look like nobody's in any hurry to leave."

"I'd better get up there. Even if this was Leslie's idea, she doesn't know what she's let herself in for."

"She'll manage," Hank said, surprisingly serious.

David glanced over at him.

"She's a fine woman, David. I admit, at first I had my doubts." He took another long, thirsty drink and set the empty bottle on the counter. "It takes guts to build a whole new life for yourself, to walk into a world that's strange to you and to learn about it instead of sitting back behind what you used to know, what you used to do, what you used to be. Leslie, now, she don't mind admitting things are strange. And when she asks you something, she don't mind listening to what you tell her and learning from what you say."

This was high praise, indeed, David recognized, from a man who seldom praised and certainly never did so just for the sake of hearing his own voice.

"She ain't Elaine, son," Hank went on solemnly. "I reckon a man is lucky to have one woman like Elaine in his life, but she's gone. And when I stopped looking for her in Leslie, I saw what you must have seen from the start. A man is just as lucky to find a woman like her. Elaine was like those race horses she loved, all sleek and showy and sure of herself. Leslie probably ain't never going to be like that. She's more like a doe, kind

of shy, real curious, and real sturdy once you look behind the softness."

*And like a doe, she'll go to any lengths to protect her
young,* David added silently. He felt his throat tightening. "What are you doing, Hank?" he asked around that
tightness. "Turning poet on me?"

"Hell, no." Hank drew the first word into two sylla-
bles as he dusted his hands on his jeans and looked
uncomfortable. "It's just that it took me a while to figure her out, to stop looking for what wasn't there and to
see what was. I reckon I came down kind of hard on her
when she first got here, and I reckon if I didn't think
apologizing would hurt her more than keeping my
mouth shut, I'd do it."

"And I *reckon*," David smiled warmly at the man
who had been his life-long friend and second father,
"that she knows you've changed your mind about her
without you having to say anything, if for no other reason than the way you've been helping her with Henry.
She's coming along fine with him, isn't she?"

Hank grinned. "Once she gets up on him."

David closed the abandoned ledgers and slid them
into the desk drawer. "Are you coming up to the
house?"

"Later," Hank told him. "After I get the last hay
trucks squared away and get cleaned up."

They left the office at the same time, pausing outside in the late afternoon heat, where David looked
toward the house and the crowd of cars belonging to
his family. He knew from long experience that Hank
was anxious to get back to work and away from his
uncharacteristic display of feelings, but there was one
more thing David had to say. "Thanks, Hank. I
needed to hear that said."

Not that it would change anything—not immediately
anyway—but he needed all the help he could get, especially since he couldn't ask for it, in unlocking the

doors to the prison he'd somehow created for himself,
and from which he couldn't escape.

Leslie stepped away from the counter and surrendered the pizza under construction to a gangly sixteen-
year-old girl with long garish red braids and braces
which flashed when she smiled. Phil's daughter, Angela, nicknamed, not unkindly, Pinkie—Leslie congrat-
ulated herself on finally being able to tie faces and
names together—the one who had supplied the rock
music that was now blaring from the stereo system at a
reasonably acceptable level of volume.

She smiled ruefully as she glanced around the huge
den and through the sliding glass doors to the pool area.
There might not be ten thousand of them, as Mike had
insisted, but there certainly were a lot of cousins, first
and second, and they weren't even all here yet. This had
been her idea: a pool and pizza party for all of the kids,
then a camping trip for the boys and a slumber party for
the girls, with the parents dropping their children off,
staying for a few minutes, and then leaving. Only no
one seemed inclined to leave. And as Leslie surveyed
the throng of people, letting their laughter and enjoyment wash over her, she discovered that she didn't want
them to leave.

She'd been concerned about Mike and Ellie. After
almost a month with no companionship other than their
own, they'd begun to get on each other's nerves, and,
with no neighbors nearby, it had seemed logical to call
on some of the family. She laughed softly. With this
much family, who needed neighbors?

And even with this much family, food had been no
problem. Once the grating, chopping, and slicing of
ingredients was finished, once her own special sauce
simmered in pans on the stove, only the assembling
and baking remained, and there were too many eager,

interested volunteers for that job for her even to get close to the oven. Mabel, as slender and wiry as Hank and usually as taciturn, was in her element, supervising the dough and preparing another huge batch because it looked as though the first huge batch she'd prepared wouldn't be enough. Grace had taken over dispensing ice and cold drinks and seeing that Leslie was introduced to everyone. And everyone else—at least the adults, because the kids were too busy catching up on each other's summer activities—after an initial period of uneasiness had set about very naturally to make Leslie feel as though she truly was welcomed into this large, noisy, boisterous, loving *family*.

David's absence was the only thing that made the gathering less than perfect. Leslie knew that he must have been detained on ranch business, but she wanted him beside her, his arm draped over her shoulder, laughing with her, sharing her happiness and showing his family that he, too, felt that she belonged. It was a futile wish. Even if he were beside her, she knew, relaxed, at ease, and, in his own caring way making sure that she felt the same, there would be no public physical display of affection. When they were alone he might, and often did, touch her, hold her, plant a surprisingly gentle kiss on her cheek or swat on her fanny, but in the presence of anyone else he maintained a distance between them. Not an aloof distance, not a cold distance, but a distance just the same.

Ellie didn't believe in maintaining a distance, though. She'd stuck to Leslie's side like a Siamese twin all afternoon, greeting the guests with her strange, adult calm and impeccable manners, refusing to leave Leslie for any reason.

"Leslie?"

Leslie heard the question in Angela's voice. She refused to call her Pinkie. Once the girl had grown out of her coltish stage and out of her braces, she was going to be breathtakingly beautiful, and she deserved some recognition and encouragement now, while she was feeling so unsure of herself. Leslie turned to answer the girl and almost fell as she tripped over Ellie.

Leslie righted herself and checked Ellie for injuries, then sighed deeply. Ellie needed recognition and encouragement, too, in being a child. But how? *How?* Surely there was something Ellie wanted to do more than hang onto her pant leg. She spotted a cousin in the corner, Brenda, a little girl of about seven or eight, who, for the moment appeared to have been forgotten by everyone else.

She knelt by Ellie. She'd tried everything else. Maybe now it was time to use the one thing she hadn't tried: Ellie's good manners. At least it wouldn't hurt anything. She turned the child toward her cousin. "I want to thank you for helping me meet all the family," she said calmly. "I wonder, though, now that I've met almost everyone, if I could ask a favor of you."

"Of course," Ellie told her.

Leslie smiled at her encouragingly. "Your cousin Brenda looks lonely. Would you mind visiting with her and making her feel at home while I see what Angela wants and then help your grandmother and Mabel in the kitchen?"

Ellie hesitated, but her innate politeness won out over her insecurity, and by the time Leslie turned her attention to Angela and the two-inch-thick creation she wanted approval for, Ellie had seated herself beside Brenda and was beginning to draw out the other little girl.

Leslie knew when David entered the room. She didn't hear him come in, she didn't see him, she *felt* him, as she always felt him—a slow, tingling awareness that spread gradually through her. She turned with a smile of welcome to see him standing on the top step near the doorway to the living room, frowning slightly as he looked over the room. She excused herself to Angela and walked to him.

"When did you decide to move the party down here?" he asked.

"When we ran out of space upstairs. David, this room is wonderful." But she felt her smile slipping as he stared with a dazed expression over the room, the long tables with their gaily checked red cloths, the throng of people wearing everything from bathing suits to business suits. Mabel had frowned when Leslie suggested moving into the den, and even Grace had seemed surprised. But Mabel had found the red gingham stored in a workroom, and Grace had pitched in with the two of them to set up the room, even to suggesting indestructible plastic glasses for the pool area and digging the paper plates and woven straw holders out of a back cabinet. Leslie had thought their initial reactions strange but had forgotten them until now. "David," she asked hesitantly. "Have I done something wrong?"

"No," he said gently. But it was several seconds before he abandoned his dazed study of the room and turned to her. "No, of course not." His expression warmed with the beginning of a smile. "I'm sorry I'm late. How are you getting along with the clan?"

"Mike!"

Leslie turned, distracted by the loud call, to see a boy about Mike's age holding a black and white soccer ball.

"Hey, Mike!" he called again and then sailed the ball across the room toward Mike where he stood near the stereo.

The ball bounced off the wall near Ellie's head, but before it could strike her, Mike snatched it up. "Watch it, sucker! You could hurt someone," Mike snarled, crouching, ready to pounce.

Leslie gasped at the animosity in her son's voice, but

before she could say anything, Ben jumped up, all appearances of judicial demeanor abandoned. "Benjamin Samuel Wilcox, you know better than to throw a ball in the house."

"Sorry, Dad," young Ben said. "Sorry, everybody," he said sheepishly. "I just wanted to know if it was your soccer ball," he said to Mike.

"Yeah. What of it?" Mike had not abandoned his stance.

"Well," Ben Junior went on, "I wanted to know if you knew how to play."

Mike began to relax, holding the ball easily in one hand. "Yeah."

"Well—" The boy was obviously ill at ease now, getting no help from Mike and all the attention of everyone else. "We"—he gestured to the group of boys near him "were wondering if you'd give us a few pointers."

Mike tossed the ball to his other hand. He did nothing so obvious as smiling, but Leslie saw the animosity fade from his eyes to be replaced with a speculative twinkle. "Yeah," he said.

There was a spattering of laughter from the rest of the kids, and conversation resumed, but as Leslie turned back to David, he surprised her by gripping her arm and nodding silently toward Mike. Mike had bent toward Ellie, and although he spoke softly, his words carried to Leslie's ears. "You okay?" She didn't hear what Ellie answered but saw Mike's hand reach out and muss her bangs. "Watch it, kid. We don't want you getting hurt by some dumb stunt like that." Then he grinned and, carrying the ball, swaggered outside.

Leslie felt moisture blurring her vision at this evidence that at last Mike and Ellie were accepting each other, that at last Mike was finding a place for himself. And what about herself? She felt David's hand burning her arm through the long-sleeved cotton shirt. Had she found a place?

"Well," she said in a small choked whisper as she turned to face David. For a moment, his face seemed to mirror her own emotions. Then, as though realizing for the first time that he was gripping her arm, he released her and let his hand fall to his side. "Well," he said uneasily, "I'd better start acting like a host."

Leslie stood at the steps and watched him as he made his way through the room, talking and laughing with his family. *A place?* Oh, yes, she had a place. But not at his side. Not when anyone else was around. She wasn't being fair to him, she knew that. He had done all he'd promised to do; he had given her all he'd promised he could give. But as Leslie stood there, alone at the stairs, surrounded by but not a part of the love that flowed through the room, she knew that it wasn't enough, would never be enough. And yet—it might be all she ever had.

She felt the pressure of unshed tears threatening her eyes and tightening her throat. She knew she couldn't stand there any longer pretending a happiness that had deserted her, and she knew that she couldn't embarrass herself or anyone else by giving vent to her emotions. As unobtrusively as possible, she slipped from the room.

Hidden away upstairs was a room obviously designed for a live-in housekeeper, comfortably furnished with a day bed and sewing machine, and equally obviously never used. This was the room Leslie had appropriated for her hideaway, creating for herself a space that was as privately hers as David's study was his, and this was the room she now sought out.

Chilled by more than air-conditioning, she opened the top half of the Dutch-style outside door and leaned against it, letting the afternoon sun bathe her with its warmth as she stared unseeingly across the tops of trees to the hazy distant mountains. The irony in her choice of a hideaway struck her for the first time. Live-in housekeeper. Live-in lover. Live in. *Live in . . . live in . . .*

"Are you all right, Leslie?"

Leslie recognized Grace's low tones. She didn't want to have to pretend for her mother-in-law, but she did. "I'm fine," she murmured, still staring out the door. "I just came upstairs for some napkins and thought I would . . ." She was horrible at lying, always had been, always would be.

"We have plenty of napkins. You just opened a new package," Grace said, moving closer to her. "What's wrong?"

Leslie turned toward her, hoping she could blame the moisture in her eyes on the brightness of the sun.

"You're in love with him, aren't you?" Grace asked.

There was no apparent censure in Grace's expression, in her voice or her words, and oh, how Leslie wanted to believe that Grace was as incapable of lying as she was.

"I could be," Leslie told the older woman finally, knowing she had to voice her thoughts to someone, "if I let myself."

Grace gave her a small, sad smile and shook her head slowly. "And why won't you let yourself?"

"You know the answer to that," Leslie said softly but squaring her shoulders in an attempt to preserve some vestige of pride. "It was one of the reasons why you opposed this marriage."

Grace said nothing, merely stood looking at Leslie patiently, questioningly, waiting.

She did know, didn't she? Leslie thought for a moment she'd been mistaken about how honest David had been with his mother, but then she remembered all the comments Grace had made and knew she hadn't been mistaken. But still Grace waited for an answer, and Leslie found she had to voice this, too. She forced her words out in a tortured whisper past the tightness in her throat. "David doesn't want me to."

She twisted away from the sight of David's mother, looking instead at the parched lawn. The last thing she expected was to feel Grace's soft touch on her shoulder, to hear Grace's voice, equally soft. "You are so young, Leslie. In spite of all you've been through. Don't you know that loving isn't a matter of *letting yourself* and *wanting to*. Oh, the outward expression of it can be. But the underlying emotion doesn't ask for permission, and denying that it exists will not make it go away."

Leslie couldn't face the woman. Grace lifted her hand, then touched her once more on the shoulder. "Come on downstairs as soon as you can," she said gently. "Eunice and her crowd have arrived, and the boys are gathering their sleeping bags, getting ready to leave."

By the time Leslie rejoined the noisy party a few minutes later, she had erased all traces of her disloyal melancholy from her expression, if not from her heart. She saw David standing with the crowd of boys, sorting out sleeping bags, and gave him a reassuring smile before going to greet his cousin Eunice and her four boys.

The boys left, piled into the jeep and a pickup truck, driven by two of them who were old enough for learner's permits but not driver's licenses, and unsupervised except by themselves. It wasn't a situation Leslie would have tolerated in New Jersey, but David had assured her the boys had been walking, riding, and driving all over these hills, and that this was nothing different from what he and his cousins had done at the same age.

The girls separated into age groups, one cluster around Angela and her stack of fashion magazines, another around Ellie and Brenda.

And still the adults showed no sign of leaving. Without any conscious effort, Leslie felt herself drawn back into the group, found herself laughing, found herself with a feeling of belonging. Almost as effortlessly, the kitchen and den were restored to their former order, with an almost imperceptible difference. Leslie had never truly felt comfortable in the big room, but now, somehow, she did.

David seemed to be waiting for something. He, Ben, and Phil were gathered near the fireplace talking, and an occasional loud laugh rang out. Only when Hank arrived, freshly scrubbed, shaved, dressed in neat jeans and a workshirt, and smelling of Old Spice, did Leslie begin to suspect what was prompting those laughs.

"How about some poker, Hank?" David asked casually while Hank downed the pizza and beer that had been set out for him.

Leslie glanced sharply at him. He smiled back at her, enjoyment in his eyes as well as conspiracy. The sight of him so totally relaxed and at ease with her took her breath away. Her protests died in her throat, and she knew then how Mike must have felt when his new cousins, who knew so much about everything else, asked him for pointers on soccer.

"You haven't played since Leslie got here," David went on. "I thought a few lessons might be in order."

Hank snorted. "Couldn't teach her yourself?" he asked.

Leslie hid her grin. "I'll get the peanuts."

Hank looked up at her startled. "I don't play for peanuts."

Ben laughed. "Come on, Hank. You can bend your rules for the first few hands, can't you? You don't want anyone taken advantage of."

Hank considered that for a moment, then looked at Leslie. "David been teaching you?" he asked.

Leslie glanced from Ben to Phil to the laughter dancing in David's eyes, making him seem younger and for the moment free of care, more *approachable*. None of this was malicious, she knew. It was a conspiracy born of love and long familiarity, a conspiracy she was being invited to join.

She looked back at Hank, fighting to keep the sheer enjoyment of the moment from bubbling forth in a revealing laugh. "Well," she said hesitantly. "We did play once, one afternoon."

"Hmpff," Hank said into his beer. "Then I suppose you do need some help. All right," he conceded. "Get the blasted peanuts. We'll use them. At least until I see how bad David's botched the job of teaching you something as important as poker."

Leslie stood on the deck outside their bedroom, letting the warm night breeze play over her as David went downstairs for one last check on the sleeping girls. She had offered to go, but, laughing, he'd stopped her. "I had enough trouble getting you away from them the first time. As much fun as you were having, one would think you'd never been to a slumber party before."

She hadn't, but that wasn't the path her thoughts were taking as she leaned against the redwood rail and listened to the night sounds, the symphony of crickets, the rustle of already dry oak leaves, the persistent, still lonely whippoorwill. How had she ever thought this place was quiet?

And how had she ever thought it was dark? A canopy of stars and a not-quite-full moon lit up the sky, bathing everything below in a silver glow. To the east, beyond the shadows she knew to be mountains, the night seemed darker, rent occasionally by a sheet of cloud-outlined lightning.

Or alien? In only a few short weeks, these mountains, this view, this place had become home for Leslie. She'd learned that she loved the rough, only partially tamed land.

She closed her eyes and leaned her head back, breathing deeply of the night as Grace's words came back to her. *Loving isn't a matter of letting yourself or wanting to.* She wanted to deny those words, but she couldn't. Not any longer. Not to herself.

How long had she loved David Nichols? Longer than this one night, when for the first time she had truly felt a part of him, a part of a family she'd always longed for but never had? Since the first time he'd made love to her, teaching her with gentleness and then passion what the physical act of love could mean? Or the few days before that, when he'd stepped gently around her shattered emotions, her doubts, her fears? Or still longer, since their first few letters when, she now knew, she'd recognized in him a need for love as great as her own but had denied that knowledge?

And what would he say when he learned that she'd lied to him about not wanting more than he could give? *That's all right, David,* she whispered silently, bitterly, *I lied to myself, too.*

She couldn't tell him, not even after the apparent closeness of this evening, not without running the risk of driving him even farther away. What she had now was what she'd only dreamed of before: a home, a family, someone who cared for her—and she knew that David did care—someone with whom to share whispered confidences, plans, disappointments, as well as the joys and responsibilities of raising their children. Loving David shouldn't destroy that, but she knew instinctively, at a level that twisted her heart, that telling him how she loved him could end it all.

She heard the whisper of drapes, soft footfalls across the deck, and then felt David's arms around her as he eased her back against him and folded his arms content-edly around her.

"They're sound asleep," he murmured near her ear.

Coming alive with the sensations David's touch never failed to evoke in her, Leslie only nodded under-standing and continued looking out across the valley.

"You're worried about Mike?"

She wasn't, hadn't been since David had assured her Mike would be all right, but that topic seemed much safer than the one her thoughts had chosen. "A little."

"He'll be fine. All of the boys have been camping since they were old enough to walk. And Eunice's twins, the boys who are driving, know these hills as well as I do. They'll be careful."

"It's just so . . . vast out there. So wild."

David laughed softly. "Believe me, the wildest things out there tonight are those boys. No self-respecting ani-mal is going to get within hollering distance of them."

Leslie hadn't even thought about that. Her earlier fears had been that they'd get lost or accidentally in-jured. "How about the not so self-respecting ones?" she asked with a suddenly dry throat. "The snakes you and Hank are always warning me about?"

"Scare tactics," he told her. "You need to be aware of them, to respect the danger they represent, but there aren't that many poisonous kinds in this area, and the ones that are here won't go out of their way to attack. Besides," he added, rubbing his hands along her arms as though sensing the chill that was running through her, "a bite can be nasty, but it doesn't always have to be fatal. All the boys know first aid and what to do in the unlikely event there's an accident."

She sighed and relaxed into his embrace. He was right, of course. This was something he knew so much more about than she did. They stood there si-lently, companionably enjoying the night, in another

shared moment, another memory for her to lock away,
until David once again began moving his hands along
her arms in a long, slow caress that had nothing to do
with chills or night breezes or fear. Her breath caught,
her heart pulled its now familiar stuttering trick, and
the surface of her skin echoed the awareness deep
within her that began with a slow, spreading warmth.
He nuzzled aside the mass of her hair, and she felt his
lips, warm and persuasive on her neck, her throat.

I love you, David Nichols, she thought as she turned
in his arms, but the only sound that escaped was a soft
moan as David covered her mouth with his and pressed
her compellingly against the length of his body. Too
soon, he dragged his mouth from hers. He caught her
face in his hands and searched for something in her
eyes, while the moon cast silver shadows across the
high planes of his cheeks, hiding his expression from
her. He gathered her to him and buried his face in her
hair.

"Leslie." It was a whispered caress, full of hunger
and anguish and something that Leslie couldn't let herself identify. Not yet. Not when it might only be her
own need demanding that she hear what wasn't there.

I love you, she repeated silently, aching to speak the
words. Instead, she turned her head, finding David's
mouth. With a groan, he crushed her to him. With his
mouth, he plundered hers, while he swept his hands
over her in a wild, searching possession. For a moment,
Leslie stiffened, frightened by David's thinly leashed,
primitive passion. Then the wildness spread to her, running through her veins and tissues like a raging brush-
fire. Her breasts throbbed against the solid wall of his
chest, against the work-roughened hands that claimed
them, abandoned them to lift her closer into him, then
returned. Her loins throbbed against the thrust of his
heated arousal through their clothing and demanded still

more closeness. Moaning, murmuring incoherent words that mingled with his, Leslie abandoned herself to David's passion—and to the searing desire he'd awakened in her—beginning to show him wordlessly what she was very much afraid he would never want her to say.

Chapter

8

DAVID LISTENED TO the low rumble of thunder and the sound of wind-driven September rain biting against the windows. He didn't have to glance at the clock to know the hour was early, but not as early as the grey light filtering into the room indicated.

He felt the whisper of Leslie's breath against his bare chest, the negligible weight of her head in the curve of his arm. She'd been asleep when he came to bed the night before, curled into herself and looking innocent and vulnerable. He had eased himself into bed beside her, careful not to disturb her. He didn't remember reaching for her, didn't know whether he'd pulled her to his side in his sleep or if she'd come to him in hers, but he'd awakened, as he always awoke now, to find his arm beneath her, holding her to him, her fingers curled loosely over his heart, her thigh resting on his. And since he was always the first to awaken, he didn't know whether she was even aware of how trustingly she slept in his arms.

He tightened his hand on the fragile bone of her shoulder. Once he would have slid his hand down her arm, to the gentle swell of her breast rising and falling with the easy cadence of her breathing; once he would have turned to watch her eyes, slumberous and already darkening with passion as they opened, to watch her lips, softening and parting with a welcoming smile, to hear her words, husky with sleep and emotion as she teased him, "The stuff that dreams are made of . . ."

Once. But not now. He willed his fingers to relax their grip on Leslie's shoulder, willed his body to be still. Now such intimacy while she slept seemed an invasion of the cloak of privacy she'd draped around her—a cloak probably imperceptible to anyone other than him, but there all the same, as it had been for a month.

The night of the party. He knew when the change had come over her. The night when his need to know Leslie as Leslie, not as a substitute for a woman who could never return, not as a temporary stand-in, not, for God's sake, as a second choice, had been so strong that he had taken her, as small and delicate as she was, with all the passion and none of the finesse of a man who'd been locked away for years.

She had responded to him, had seemed, at the time, to match his wildness, and had denied that he hurt her. But since that time she hadn't been as open with him, as free—almost as though she were guarding her words and actions to prevent a repetition of that night.

There wouldn't be one. He wasn't a violent man; he wasn't a man who couldn't control his emotions. But she had no way of knowing that. He couldn't tell her;

he'd have to show her that she had nothing to fear from him.

He shifted his arm, preparing to rise. Leslie turned in her sleep, snuggling closer into him. Her lips brushed his flesh as she murmured a sleepy protest; her thigh moved in innocent provocation over his as she settled back into sleep.

David fought back a swift jolt of desire. Remaining motionless, fighting his body's responses, he waited until Leslie's breathing told him she had slipped more deeply into sleep. Then, easing his arm from beneath her, he rose from the bed and began dressing for the day that he'd promised himself he would not let disturb him.

Leslie awoke the moment David took his arm from her, watching him through shuttered lids and feeling his warmth slowly slipping away from her.

I love you, she thought silently, as she thought silently every morning, every evening. How long could she remain silent? How long could she hide from him something that he didn't want? *As long as I have to,* she told herself, although, except for rare moments, it seemed like that might be forever.

She wanted to call him back to the bed—her awakening body demanded it; her soul cried out for his closeness, for the semblance of caring—but she saw his face in the mirror as he passed before it, his beautiful, chiseled features taut with tension, and once again kept silent. He'd told her the night before he would be facing a long and trying day. And already he was preparing for that day, leaving her in the background where she would remain until after the children were in bed that evening and she had to resume the charade of not loving him.

David stopped at the door and turned to look at her. Leslie steadied her breathing, simulating sleep. After a moment, David turned again and let himself quietly out of the room.

As early as he was, David found Hank already in the barn when he arrived. The horses had been fed, and Hank was deftly repairing the cinch of a light-weight bareback pad he'd unearthed from somewhere in the depths of the tack room.

David eyed the pad suspiciously. "Are the cattle penned?"

"Yep," Hank said around a wad of snuff. "You knowed that."

"And Jake and Hal know what time to be here?"

"Yep." Hank spit a stream of tobacco juice at a waiting can. "You knowed that, too."

For several minutes, David paced restlessly through the organized clutter in the end of the barn that was undisputedly Hank's domain. Finding nothing to do, he turned back to Hank and his project. "What's that for?"

"Leslie," Hank said without looking up from his work. "It won't help her to mount—she's still going to need a fence rail or a tree stump—but with this she can ride without having to wait for one of us to hoist a saddle up on Henry for her."

"No." David spoke sharply, too sharply, he knew, when Hank glanced up with an unspoken question in his eyes.

"That's a good way to get her hurt," David said. "She doesn't have any business riding without one of us with her, and she damn sure doesn't have any business trying to control Henry with nothing more substantial than that . . ." he glanced disparagingly at the pad as his words trailed off.

Hank shot another stream of tobacco at the can and resumed work. "What time is Johnson coming out?"

David felt himself drawing away from the question,

an apparent change of subject that wasn't really. Hank knew him too well. "Before noon."

"You ought to sell that damn thing. Either fly it or sell it. It ain't doing nobody no good sitting up there ruining. Just reminding you. And you don't need that."

"And I don't need you telling me what to do—" David fought for control, stunned by the violence in his voice, stunned by his reaction to Hank's all-too-true comment.

"That's all right, boy," Hank said, putting the pad aside and stretching his creaking knees. "I've got a tough old hide. I see more than you think I see, and I hear more than you say. But some folks around here don't have thirty-five years of knowing you to fall back on. They don't know nothing but what you show them. What are you showing them these days?"

What was he showing them? Too close to his own thoughts that morning, Hank's question troubled him. Not only Leslie. David knew that Hank included her but that his concern also encompassed Ellie and Mike. "All that I can," he said. Then, when Hank continued to watch him, he did his best to hide his doubts that "all he could" was enough and found a smile for the man who could be maddeningly perceptive at times and maddeningly obtuse at others.

"Don't you have something you need to do?"

"Nope." Hank settled himself back onto the bale of hay and pulled the bareback pad to him. "Not until it stops raining. But I reckon," he said as he bent his head to his work, "that your wife ought to have breakfast about ready by now. You've got time on your hands. Why don't you spend it with your family?"

The rain had slowed to a heavy mist by the time David reached the house. It hadn't been much of a rain, in spite of its early threat, accomplishing not much more than pasting yellow leaves to the cars and exposed farm vehicles. Once the sun came out, the only reminder of what could have been a storm would be the steam rising in the heat, and a little mud—not much—in the pens where they would vaccinate a select herd of calves.

He heard laughter as he approached the doors to the breakfast room, and for a moment a wave of desolation washed over him. *His family?* Elaine and Tommy and Ellie were his family. A family that had been violently severed. A family that he should have been able to protect. He pushed those thoughts aside. Ellie was his family now. She waited inside those doors, needing him now more than she ever had. And Leslie. And Mike.

He opened the door and stepped inside. Leslie, in the process of bending over the table, looked up at him, and her face softened in a warm, welcoming smile. Ellie turned to him, calling "Daddy!" Even Mike, caught in the aftermath of laughter, seemed to be smiling at him. Their warmth was as real as the heady aromas of food drifting from the kitchen table, seeming to reach out and envelop him. He paused for a moment, savoring the feeling and the sight that he had looked at countless times in the past but had never really seen. Then he felt his own answering smile gentling his features. He closed the door behind him, took off his hat and tossed it onto a nearby chair. "Did you save anything for me?"

Leslie produced a plate and silverware and a cup of steaming coffee for him. Mike and Ellie, remembering their manners, began passing platters of hotcakes, bacon, and eggs, and, without more than a moment's hesitation, conversation resumed around the table, drawing him in, weaving its spell around him and through him.

Ellie sparkled. Prim and neatly dressed as always, there was an animation, a liveliness about her that he'd sorely missed during the past two years. He shot a glance of appreciation at Leslie, knowing it was her influence more than his that had brought about this change in his daughter, but Leslie was busy choking back a laugh at some absurdly mature comment of Ellie's and didn't see his look.

Mike asked him a question, and, grateful that this time he knew the answer, David answered. It was a start, he thought. Mike had begun reaching out, questioning, seeking advice. More often than not, he turned to Hank, as David had done when he was a child, but lately he'd also made some tentative overtures toward David and had been more open to, if not totally accepting of, the overtures David made toward him.

"Okay, kids," Leslie said with gentle firmness. "You're going to miss the school bus if you don't get a move on."

"It's still raining," David said, exaggerating the moisture clouding the windows. "Why don't I drive you to the bus stop?"

"All right!" Mike jumped up from the table. "Will you let me drive?"

"Mike." Leslie's calm voice interrupted his plea.

"Oh, all right. I'll get my books," he said and started from the room.

"Mike?" she repeated.

He returned to the table, sighed in heavy frustration, picked up his dishes and carried them into the kitchen.

Ellie stood up, pushed in her chair, and then in fierce imitation, sighed deeply, picked up her dishes and followed Mike.

David's eye caught Leslie's as the children left to gather books, and silently they shared a moment of understanding. Their children were accepting each other. Ellie hadn't simply transferred her allegiance from him to Leslie and then to Mike; she had widened that allegiance to include all of them. And Mike, for all of his gruff talk about "the kid," ate up the affection she gave him.

Leslie smiled. For a moment David saw more in her smile than understanding. For a moment he saw longing, unspoken questions, and hesitation. Then she shook her head slightly, gathered their plates and walked into the kitchen.

David picked up two platters and followed her, entering the kitchen in time to hear the crash of breaking glass and Leslie's muffled oath. He hurriedly found a place for the platters on the cabinet and turned toward Leslie. A plate lay in shards in the sink, and blood welled from a slash on her finger. He snatched up her hand, turning on the cold water to wash the wound, feeling her stiffen against his touch. A sliver of china protruded from the cut. With deft fingers he removed it.

"I'm sorry about the plate," Leslie said in a tight voice.

"You don't think I'm worried about the plate, do you?" he asked, but a glance at her wide, shadowed eyes confirmed that she did. Why? he asked himself. *Why?* What had he ever done to make her think that he cared more for the possessions in this house than the people? But then, he realized, what had he ever done to make her think otherwise?

He felt her tremble and turned her to face him. "Leslie, plates are just things. Like everything else in this house, they're meant to be used and enjoyed. Damn it! You could have hurt yourself." He still held her hand. *"This* is important," he said, lifting her finger to his lips. *"You* are important." As he spoke, he recognized the truth of his words. She was important to him and had been for longer than he'd realized.

He drew her finger into his mouth, exploring its soft texture with his teeth and tongue, aware of the sensations that the taste and feel of her awoke in his mouth, in every nerve of his body. Slowly he slid his other arm around her. Easing back against the cabinet, he drew her into the cradle of his hips. He felt her shudder and relax against him, resting her hand at his waist and then clutching him as she turned her face toward his.

Desire flowed through him, hot and sweet, but along with desire, something else, a need to protect her, to comfort her. He released her hand, felt it sliding to cup his cheek, and enfolded her in his arms. "Oh, Leslie," he asked wonderingly, "what do you do to me?"

"We're ready."

David glanced up at the hesitant intrusion. Mike and Ellie stood in the doorway, Ellie grinning, Mike looking steadily at the refrigerator. Leslie jumped at his voice and tried to pull away from David. He let her go, but only a little way.

He looked once again at the children and then at the flushed, embarrassed expression on the face of the woman in his arms. He had tiptoed around the children for two months, not knowing how either of them, but especially Mike, would react to intimacies between the two of them. He still didn't know. Twice he'd been involved in silent confrontations with Mike, wordless challenges in which Mike seemed bent on proving to him that Leslie loved him more than she loved David. David had backed away each time, knowing the futility of becoming embroiled in useless arguments with his adopted son, especially when, if Mike only knew it, there could be no contest. But, damn it, he wanted to kiss his wife. His wife. Once Leslie had reminded him that she was his wife. Then it had been only a word, a label, with subtly altered meaning. When had the meaning evolved? For a moment he looked at her with new vision. From the look of her, from the response she had given him only a few moments before, she'd wanted to kiss him, too. At least she *had* wanted to. And after what Mike and Ellie had witnessed, one kiss could do no more harm.

It wasn't the kind of kiss he would have given her had they not been interrupted, but in an unidentifiable way it was still satisfying. Placing his hands on her shoulders, he bent and brushed her lips in a chaste, closed-mouth whisper. She looked up at him, and her eyes flooded with surprise and wonder.

"We'll be working cattle later this morning," he told her softly. "Would you like to watch?"

When she hesitated, obviously bemused, he smiled. "Hank's looking forward showing off for you. And besides, with you there, he'll keep his language clean enough not to scare off the two new hands we've hired."

Rewarded by her answering smile, he squeezed her shoulders and released her. "Okay, you two," he said to the waiting audience, "let's get going."

Hank wanted to show off for her? Leslie thought as she leaned back against the barn and watched the riders herding the milling cattle from the catch pen where they'd spent the night toward the working pens. David saw her and rising gracefully in the saddle, waved his hat. Grinning, still wrapped in the unexpected magic of their shared morning, Leslie nodded but made no movement that would spook the approaching cattle.

Rather than stationary fences, the pens were made up of a bewildering assortment of metal gates that could be opened or closed to create alleys, traps, or freedom. In the center of one was a long, fixed alley ending in a metal, hand-operated mechanical contraption—a squeeze chute, David had told her, and head gate—where each individual cow could be herded and restrained while being treated.

The men were off their horses now, separating the bawling, irate mother cows from the calves, and Leslie knew that any movement she made wouldn't be noticed. She climbed onto the top rail of a fence, hooked her tennis shoes around another rail, and perched there watching, fascinated.

The two new hands David had told her about touched

their hats in acknowledgment of her, Hank nodding in her direction. After the cattle were separated, David walked over to her, smiling.

"Is this place all right?" she asked. "I won't be in the way?"

"It's fine. But if you want, you can come down in the pen with us."

Leslie glanced at the trapped calves, already pushing each other into the alley that would lead them to the squeeze chute, at the men, and at the array of medication and paraphernalia laid out and waiting. "I think I'll stay up here."

David dropped his hands to the rails on each side of her, and Leslie breathed in the warmth of him, the nearness of him. Whatever had caused it, the morning's magic was still with them.

Leslie heard the clang of metal, the outraged bawl of a calf, and Hank's rough voice. "Hey, Doc! You want us to start without you?"

David's smile became a rueful grin as he straightened away from her, turned, walked to the side of the chute and picked up an instrument that looked like a cross between a stainless steel syringe and a deadly weapon. But there was little time for smiling, grinning, or even noticing her once the work began.

The four men functioned as an efficient team, making quick work of vaccinating, dusting, spraying, inspecting, and releasing each animal. Leslie was marveling at the speed and ease with which they worked together when she became aware of another man approaching. He walked up to the fence and hooked his arms over the top rail.

"Morning, Mrs. Nichols," he said companionably, looking at the activity in the pens.

"Good morning," Leslie answered, wondering if she should know him. He didn't look like a cousin, although he was tall and slender, and, in spite of his jeans and boots, he didn't look like a ranch hand. He wore a baseball cap with the logo *Johnson Aviation* over thinning black hair.

"Are they going to be much longer?"

"I don't think so."

There was a lull in activity as one calf scrambled from the chute. The man beside her raised his arm and waved. "Yo! David!"

David looked up, obviously hot and tired, and incongruously dusty in spite of the mud that caked his boots and the lower legs of his jeans. His features froze in the beginning of a questioning glance, then tightened. Seeming almost to steel himself for a confrontation, he handed the syringe to Hank and walked to them.

"Morning, Ken," he said emotionlessly. "Have you met my wife?"

Ken grinned good-naturedly. "Not officially."

David didn't return his smile. "Leslie, this is Ken Johnson."

"Did I come at a bad time?"

"No."

Leslie saw a bleakness in David's expression before he masked it.

"No," he repeated. "We might as well get started." He glanced up at Leslie, and she could see no expression in his eyes, not irritation, anger, frustration, interest—nothing. "This may take a while," he said before he eased through a gate and walked away with Ken Johnson.

"Leslie." Leslie turned at Hank's curiously gentle voice to see that he had walked to her side while she watched David leave.

"Why don't you come on down and help us?"

"Help you?" she asked. "Me? You know how much I know about cows."

He stood back, studying her. "You know enough to

hand me supplies. With David gone, we could use another pair of hands."

"You'll continue?" she asked, surprised. "Without him?"

"Oh hell—heck, Leslie. It don't take no fancy vet degree to do what we're doing. Cowmen have been doing it for years."

Leslie grinned, in spite of her worry about David, at the indignation in the older man's voice.

"He just likes to keep an eye on us," Hank continued. "Especially since this herd is his latest project."

"Project?" she asked, intrigued by the emphasis Hank had put on the word.

"A new crossbreed he's been developing. Looks like he's finally come up with what he wants. 'Course, we won't know for sure until these calves mature and have calves of their own."

Fascinated, Leslie slipped from the fence. She knew that she had to take a closer look at David's work, even if it meant walking among the animals, but she couldn't easily dismiss David's reaction to Ken Johnson.

"Hank," she asked hesitantly, "who was that man?"

Hank reached for the ever-present round, flat can of snuff in his shirt pocket, glanced at her, and then replaced the can, unopened. "Johnson?" She nodded. "Airplane mechanic. David won't sell that son-of-a-buck up there in the hangar. Says he might need it some day. So it sits there, and every once in a while Johnson comes out and flies it, and once a year he gives it the inspection the law says it has to have."

"David doesn't fly it? Ever?"

"Not anymore. Never saw a boy take to anything the way he took to flying. He used to spend almost as much time in the air as he spent on the ground, but a man don't walk away from a crash like that one without some scars, even if they don't show. He ain't flown since."

Leslie felt the blood draining from her. She grasped a fence rail, staring at Hank. *A crash like that one?* Hank could be talking about only one crash. David had been there? Elaine had been killed in a crash of *her* plane. Tommy had died in the same crash. Ellie had been injured. That was what he'd told her. That was enough, more than enough, to scar a man. But to have been there? Not once had he given her any indication that he had been.

She heard her voice, thready, forced, hesitant. "David wasn't . . . the pilot?"

"No." Then, as though realizing he'd led her into strange, dangerous territory, he took a step away from her. "No," he repeated. He glared at the syringe he held, then thrust at her. "We got calves to work. I'd appreciate your help."

This may take a while, David had told her. And it did. All morning. Through lunch. Into the afternoon. *God,* Leslie thought as she waited in the silent house for his return, *why hadn't he told her?*

The summons of the telephone was only a mild irritation until she answered it and heard a strange, male voice. "Mrs. Nichols, this is Brad Hill, principal of the junior high school. I hate to bother you, ma'am, but would you mind coming to my office?"

"Is something wrong?" Leslie asked hurriedly. Had Leta and Harrison Burgess found Mike? she thought in the few seconds it took to speak.

"It's Mike and Ellie," the man said tiredly. "They've been in a fight."

A few minutes later, on her way to the school, the magic of the morning hung in crystal shards around her. Leslie choked back a bitter laugh that threatened to disintegrate into a sob. There had been hope for her and David that morning; she had felt it, alive, growing, real, in everything that had happened since he walked into the breakfast room, but now... She could hide her love from him for as long as necessary, she could hide her hurt that he'd kept from her something as important as the knowledge that he'd been in the crash that killed his wife and son, could even find some reason to justify his holding that secret to himself, if she searched hard and long enough. But Mike and Ellie... Aside from the problems this fight would cause the two children, aside from the underlying problems that had caused the fight—

She gripped the steering wheel and tried to concentrate on the road. Would Mike now renew his efforts to return to his grandparents? Would Ellie revert to the shadow of the child she'd been?

And faced with more complications than he needed, would David decide their arrangement just wasn't working? He wouldn't ask her to leave, she knew that. David was an honorable man. She almost choked on the word honorable. She didn't want his honor; she wanted his love. But under the terms of their contract, that wasn't an option, probably would never be an option now. And under the terms of the contract—she recalled each phrase with startling, chilling clarity—she was there for only two significant purposes: to act as a mother for Ellie, helping her recover from the trauma of her loss and injury and become once again the daughter David knew she was, and to provide him a substitute son for the one he'd lost. And from the looks of things, in spite of her hopes, in spite of the progress she thought she'd made with the children, she was failing miserably in both her allotted roles.

Chapter

9

DAVID LET HIMSELF into the house through the front door. Without the energy for the toss he'd perfected over the years, he hung his hat on the hall tree and leaned back against the doorway.

Leslie hadn't physically changed anything in the house. All the possessions so carefully selected and placed by Elaine were just as carefully tended by Leslie. And yet, everything about the house had changed. No longer simply a beautiful setting, for the first time in as long as he could remember, his house felt like a home.

He supposed it was natural for his thoughts to turn to Elaine. Working with the airplane always brought his simmering memories to the forefront. And he supposed he ought to take Hank's advice and sell the plane.

Would that help? He dropped his head in his hands and massaged his forehead. Would anything help?

God, he was tired. Tired of the relentless vision of the last time he'd seen Elaine and Tommy, tired of hurting, tired of telling himself that no matter what he knew now, there was nothing he could have done at the time to change what happened.

He raised his head. Downstairs, the comfortable curved sectional couch beckoned him. What would happen if he just collapsed on it, mud and all? Elaine would have been appalled. Possessions had been important to her, and although she worked willingly by his side, the taint of horse, cow, or dirt was never allowed inside her house. Leslie, on the other hand—he found a smile tugging his mouth at the thought. If Leslie found him collapsed on the couch in his muddy work clothes, what would she do? Ask him about his day? Help him with his boots? Offer to bring him iced tea? Probably all three, David realized.

And there was the difference between the two women. Elaine had constantly challenged him with her quick wit, her beauty, and her varied, demanding interests. Life with her, while at times exhausting, had never been uneventful. Leslie, with her quiet ways, her soft laughter, her enjoyment in learning, and her open, delighted responses to his lovemaking, gave him something that in eleven years of marriage he had never found with Elaine, something that, until he experienced it, he hadn't even realized he needed. Leslie gave him peace.

David shook his head and then looked around as though waking up from a long and troubled sleep. Then with a determined step, he headed upstairs, to the shower, knowing that he had to wash away a lot more than mud.

Later, in his study, surrounded by the organized clutter of high school athletic trophies, academic awards, well-read books, and furniture chosen for comfort more than for style, David acknowledged another truth about his house, one he had begun to learn as he paced the silent halls after his shower. Leslie was gone. The missing Buick told him that she must have thought of some errand she needed to run. But without her presence, the house was just a house, a collection of beautifully furnished, empty rooms.

He heard the faint sound of a car pulling onto the graveled drive and found himself relaxing into his chair. Leslie was home.

He heard the front door open, footsteps on the stairs, and then, as though she'd known instinctively where he was, he saw her framed in the doorway of his study.

"David." The forced calmness in her voice and in her expression stopped his welcoming smile and his step toward her. "We have a problem."

They had a number of problems, not the least of which was the need, he now recognized, to reevaluate their marriage, their hopes for the future.

"I'm sorry to bother you with it," she went on, unmindful of the confusion her words caused him. "I ought to be able to handle it myself, I know, and if it were only Mike involved I'd know how—"

Mike. He felt the remnants of his smile fading along with the enthusiasm he'd so briefly felt and remembered the distance she'd maintained for the past month. Her son. Her reason for being here.

"—but it concerns Ellie, too." Her words had all come out in a rush. She paused for breath and looked up at him, pleading with her eyes for an understanding he didn't have. "I need your help."

"It sounds serious," he said softly, questioningly. Ominous, he thought. Not once since she'd arrived had she asked him to help her with anything.

"It is." She swallowed once and then charged on.

"Mike and Ellie have been in a fight." She threw a hand in front of her as if to hold him still. "Not with each other. Together."

Now it was David's turn to draw a deep breath. Nothing she could have said would have shocked him more. "How are they?"

"Basically, they're all right."

"Where are they?"

"In the living room."

"Do you know what happened?"

She sagged against the doorway with such obvious relief that he wondered if she'd thought he would charge after the children like some mad bull, but he had only a moment to wonder why she should think such a thing.

"Oh, yes," she said. "I heard the whole story. But not from them. Both of them are being remarkably silent on the subject. A teacher witnessed everything, she just wasn't able to get there in time to do more than break it up."

"Go on," he prompted gently. He wasn't surprised that Mike had been in a fight. Mike had been spoiling for one for days. He'd been leery of Mike's reaction to the scene in the kitchen that morning. For a moment he had been afraid that the fight was that reaction. But Ellie had been in a fight, too? *Ellie?* And *together?*

"It took place at the end of the lunch hour. Mike and a couple of boys were horsing around with the soccer ball. Ellie had wandered over from her playground— you know how Ellie is?"

He nodded. When Ellie attached to someone, she didn't let minor things like school boundaries deter her.

"She was standing on the sidelines, near where the boys had left their books. An older boy—Will Hastings?"

"I know Will," David told her. Will was at least two years older and about ten inches taller than Mike. "I also know Will's dad."

Leslie looked up at him, her lips quirking, but she controlled herself. "Will took the soccer ball away from the boys and refused to give it back. Apparently he taunted them pretty badly, but the teacher says that none of them did anything she wouldn't have done in a similar situation. Then he must have spotted Ellie. He said something to the effect that they were just a bunch of sissies who wouldn't fight, and if they were going to act like girls, he'd just give the ball to one of them. He threw the ball at Ellie, hard enough to knock her down—"

"Oh, God. Her back?"

"She's not hurt," Leslie told him. She shuddered and tried to smile. "You're not going to think so when you see her, but the school nurse checked her thoroughly, and she's not hurt. Anyway, that's when Mike tackled Will. Without a word. Just flailed into him with hands and feet and, I'm not sure, but maybe teeth, too, and that's when the teacher decided, finally, that she'd better do something. Only she was too late to do much.

"Will is bigger than Mike," she said apologetically.

"Will is much bigger than Mike," he told her. "It had to be an awfully one-sided fight."

"That's what Ellie must have thought." Leslie hesitated.

"Go on."

"She picked up one of the books at her feet and waded in to help."

David closed his eyes, trying to block out the vision of his tiny daughter caught between two angry, fighting boys.

"There's more, isn't there?" he asked.

Leslie looked at him, her eyes sparkling. "I'm not sure you're ready to hear this, but we may have a hospital bill to pay."

Because of her frailty, David's concern had immediately been for Ellie. Now, belatedly, he remembered his other child, an adopted son who hadn't hesitated to tackle someone half again his weight in defense of a little girl he had known for only two months. "Mike?" he asked. "But you told me they were all right."

Leslie was grinning, definitely grinning, although she tried to fight it. "Will." She shook her head, losing her battle for control. "Ellie took him out. When he came to, they carted him off to the emergency room. He has three stitches in his scalp."

"Ellie? Took him out? Will Hastings?" David said, disbelieving, dazed.

Leslie walked to him, stopping in front of him, reaching out for him but not touching him. When she looked up at him, tears sparkled on her lashes. "I hate fighting. I hate violence of any kind, but I'm so proud of the two of them, I don't know what to do. Whether to swat them or hug them. Whether to shout or sing. You know what this means, don't you?"

Yes, he knew. He lifted his hand to Leslie's cheek. She let it rest there for only a moment before stepping uneasily away from him. He knew what that meant, too. Their children had accepted each other, bonded together in a way he had never imagined possible, but a chasm still yawned between him and Leslie.

Leslie lay in the darkness, watching the unyielding wall of David's back. After what seemed like hours, he had finally come to bed, but for the first time since their sham of a marriage began, he turned on his side, away from her. Now, ages later, he lay unnaturally still, locked in the grip of a tension she could only begin to fathom.

His tension had to have its source in the memories the airplane evoked, in a pain so great he hadn't even been able to mention it to her. He needed to talk—she knew that from her own experience—needed to work through his grief and anger and fear, the way he had urged Ellie to do, the way Madge had forced Leslie to do. Leslie had had the added burden of guilt when Michael was killed, fostered by Leta Burgess's accusations, fed by her own insecurities. Michael hadn't been on his way to the grocery store, to run an errand that she'd been too lazy or too disorganized to have done herself, as Leta had insisted. They'd been fighting. Bitterly. As they'd begun, too often, to fight. And Michael had stormed out of the apartment, headed for a destination that, for Mike's sake, and for the sake of the love she'd once felt for Michael, she had kept silent about— a place where he'd been spending most of his time since losing his last job, a local bar three doors down from the grocery. He had gotten as far as the grocer's when the two robbers, only kids, not even old enough to buy the liquor they had drunk, panicked in their robbery attempt and started shooting.

Leslie had run the whole range of guilt when Michael died. *If* they hadn't fought. *If* she had been more supportive of Michael, more understanding. *If* she had never entered his life. Madge had dragged it all from her, made her examine it, helped her to realize that Michael had had choices, too, that Leslie hadn't forced him out of the house and couldn't be held responsible, not even by herself, for what had happened to him.

Leslie had shared only part of that with David. She'd share it all if she thought it would help him now, but she didn't think it would. He had effectively closed her out. Throughout the remainder of the afternoon and interminably long evening, she had sensed him pulling away from her, drawing into a shell of his own making where she was not welcome or needed. Throughout the afternoon and evening, Leslie had tried to maintain a facade of indifference, denying her own hurt as she tended to the needs of the children, laughing with them, easing them into bed, relying on weeks of role playing and her own recent bitter remembrance of what her role actually was to sustain her.

No, Leslie thought, still watching him in the dark, David wouldn't talk to her; he would probably resent any effort on her part to get him to do so. But there was something she could do for him, *if* he would let her. She could help him, for a brief time at least, to forget.

For hours she had fought the need to touch him, to hold him; now, her decision made, she found she had to force her hand to move. She didn't know how to do this. She had always responded to David's lovemaking, at first with a passion that both surprised and frightened her, then with a growing freedom and joy, but she had never instigated it. She wasn't a seductress, and in spite of the names that still rose from the depths of her memory, although rarely, now, she didn't know how to be one.

Love, she thought. *With* love and *in* love. And if he rejected her? Leslie pushed that thought away. Her pride had taken batterings before; it would again. Whether David knew it or not, whether he ever acknowledged it or not, tonight he needed her, and, she admitted with a silent moan deep within her, tonight she needed him.

She lifted her hand to his shoulder. Beneath supple skin, tight muscles bunched and flinched from her touch. Leslie closed her eyes for a moment, steeling herself against his unspoken rejection. "David," she said softly. "Hold me. Please."

For long seconds, he remained still. Then, slowly, he turned toward her, gathering her in the loose embrace of his arm and settling her head in the hollow of his shoulder. His head was above hers, on the pillow, and Leslie knew without looking that he wasn't watching her but was staring into the darkness of the night at things she couldn't see.

"Can't you sleep, either?" he asked gently.

She nestled closer to the body she had come to need

so much, the *man* she had come to love so well, her senses filled with the texture of him, the clean, heady, male scent of him. "No."

She felt his hand on her head, his fingers in her hair, stroking her, absently, without passion, without any intent to arouse her. But with David, she didn't need his intent. She felt her body tightening. Carefully, she dropped her hand to his chest, imitating his easy stroking.

"And what goblins are running through your mind tonight?" he asked her.

"Dreams," she told him, deliberately giving a lighter meaning to her honest answer. "Fantasies."

His hand stilled. "Fantasies, Leslie?" he asked in his night-quiet voice. "You?"

Even me, she thought at the soft surprise in his voice. *Especially me.* Beginning a delicate tracing of circles on his smooth chest, she kept her voice light, emotionless. "Of course, me. All women have them. Usually, if they'll admit it, about someone tall, dark, and handsome." She punctuated her statement by finishing a circle and sliding her fingertip down his chest, stopping a scant inch above his navel.

She felt him shudder, heard his quick intake of breath. "Leslie," he said in a voice not quite so steady, "in the first place, I'm not tall—"

Ease up, she told herself. *Don't brood all over this man. He doesn't need it. Not tonight.* She raised herself on her elbow to look up at him. Even lying beside him, she had to bend her head backwards to make contact with his dark eyes—eyes which at last were turned toward her in what appeared to be questioning concentration. She let her mouth soften into the smile it wanted to form. "That depends on your perspective," she said. "From where I stand, you look awfully tall."

Rewarded by his answering smile, she eased back against his chest, feathering a kiss over the velvet flesh resting beneath her lips. He brought his other arm to her back, holding her there, igniting small fires along her spine with his trailing fingers. "With you, sometimes I feel tall," he admitted to the air above her head.

Leslie sighed and let her hand move where it would, across his chest, down his side, tracing the lean musculature covering his ribs, to his flank.

"And in your fantasies"—David drew a shaky breath as her fingers came to rest on his thigh—"what happens?"

"I don't think I can tell you," Leslie whispered. "They're so personal." She let her fingers begin moving again, in fascinated exploration of the textures beneath them, the light furring of hair on the smooth skin of his thigh, the strength of muscle and sinew, growing taut beneath her touch. "I might—" Now it was time for her breath to catch as he tightened his hands on her back and shifted slightly, bringing her breasts into contact with the solid haven of his chest. "I might be able to show you, though."

His voice was no more than a low groan in the darkness. "Show me, Leslie."

Show me, Leslie. He wasn't going to reject her. She released tightly held breath and relaxed against him. But now what did she do? Unthinking need had carried her this far, but now her mind was alive with thoughts, with doubts. Could she please him? Foolish, foolish woman, she realized. In long nights of loving, David had taught her what pleasured her, had shown her what pleased him. Leslie knew that she only had to remember one other thing: *with* love, and *in* love, as she began sharing with him the knowledge he had so gracefully given her, as she began learning with touch and taste the secrets of his body as he had long ago learned the secrets of hers.

The ridge of his ribs, the flat hardness of his belly, the strength of his thighs, the curve of a calf, the surprisingly fine bones of his feet, all of these new discoveries fascinated her, delighted her, invited her renewed curiosity on the lingering, return journey.

David lay still beneath Leslie's touch, open to her discoveries, with only a restless shifting of his body, increasingly labored breathing, betraying how affected he was, until her lips returned to the soft flesh of his inner thigh. Her cheek brushed against him, erasing forever any doubt that she pleased him. He caught her head with both hands, tangling his fingers in her hair. She knew what he wanted, knew what she would do, but not just yet.

Relentlessly she moved on, lips and teeth and tongue marking a path across his thigh, to his hip, to his belly, while her hands charted matching paths along his hips, his buttocks, his back. Only then did she surrender to what his restless hands, his harsh breathing pleaded for, and then only instinct guided her as she slid her hand down his side and up along his thigh to cup the waiting fullness. Only instinct guided the tentative touch of her fingers, her lips.

David moaned, an indistinct murmur that could have been her name, and his fingers tightened in her hair, emboldening her. She hadn't thought to derive pleasure from this, only to return some of the pleasure he had given her, but in that thought, as in so many others, she had been wrong. He was so vulnerable, so trusting in this most intimate of caresses. Once again she let instinct guide her, instinct and the growing hunger deep within her, as she deepened the caress, losing herself in the sensations which flooded through her, until she realized his restless movements were becoming demanding. Reluctantly, she pulled away from him, resting her cheek on his belly while she stilled her breathing.

She felt his hands on her shoulders, pulling her upward. She wanted to surrender to him, to still the clamoring of her own nerves, but she resisted, shaking her head. This night was for him, too, not just her.

"The thing with fantasies," she said between her own labored breaths, "is that they tend to go on forever. Like this." She eased her weight onto him, cradling his arousal with her own heated flesh, and, dipping her head to his chest, she began exploring it as thoroughly as she had the rest of his body, working her entranced way over his rib cage, the smooth muscles of his chest, circling his flat male nipples with her tongue and feeling the shudder run through him, to the pulse beating madly in his throat, to the hollow behind his ear, ever aware of the tension mounting in him—a new tension, one caused by the pleasure she was giving him—his body arching beneath hers, the tremor in his arms caused by the strain of not crushing her to him.

She hesitated when she reached his mouth, her lips a breath away from his, and looked into his eyes. His features were tight with strain, his eyes hooded, his mouth parted slightly. He raised his hand to her cheek, and even in the fleeting touch of his fingers, she felt him tremble.

"This is your fantasy," he murmured. "What happens next?"

"This—" Leslie bit off her words. *This is when you tell me you love me,* she had almost said. But she could never say that, could never let him know she wanted more from him than what she had. Appalled by her near betrayal, she could only look at him, at the features that had become so dear to her, at soft brown eyes she would never be able to fathom the depths of. "I—"

"This?" he asked, cupping her face and bringing her mouth to his, plundering it with still leashed restraint but releasing her own clamoring needs until she forgot everything but the hot desire racing through her, demanding fulfillment.

"What next?" he whispered against her throbbing mouth.

"I—" Leslie could barely speak, could barely think. "I'm working on it."

"Ah, Leslie, surely you don't have fantasies in which you give everything, receive nothing."

Nothing? He thought she had received nothing? But before she could deny that, David tightened his arms around her and moved, shifting them so that now she was beneath him, cradling but not crushed by his weight.

"Surely in your fantasy," he whispered as his clever lips and tongue moved down her throat, "there's room for this?" He cupped her breasts with his palms, moving his hands in slow circles until his teasing mouth reached its destination.

"Yes," Leslie said, gasping, as he drew the tip of her already throbbing breast into his mouth.

His hands moved over her body, inflaming already ignited fires, tracing an ever lower path, until he found her moist warmth. "And this?"

"Oh, yes," she moaned, arching into his touch, her body on fire and screaming for him.

"And"—his mouth left her breast, moved with deliberate slowness over her, across her ribs, across her belly; he slid his hands beneath her, lifting her to him—"this?"

"God, yes." Leslie's thin cry was choked from her by the rasp of his tongue. Tremors shook her as his kiss became less gentle, more demanding, until she heard herself crying out his name in mindless litany, felt herself perched on the edge of an abyss with nothing to keep her from going over but the clutch of her fingers in his hair. "David . . ."

Reluctantly he drew away from her and looked up at her. "The thing about fantasies," he repeated breathlessly, dazed, almost as lost as she was, "is that they tend to go on forever. I'm just a man, Leslie. I need you. Now."

And she needed him. Opening her arms, she drew him into her body, into her heart.

David looked down at the woman curled trustingly against him, her head on his shoulder, her hand over his heart, her thigh resting on his. Leslie wasn't asleep, but he knew she was so close to sleep that it would be only a matter of moments before she slipped away from him.

She had done it again, shown him a piece of heaven he hadn't even known he'd missed. He didn't want to lose her to sleep. As drained as he was, as replete as he was, what he wanted to do was hold her to him until his body recovered and they could once again reenter the world unlocked by Leslie's fantasy.

He certainly didn't want to do what he knew he had to do next. But unless he did, their fantasy world would remain just that. Fantasy. And David knew now that an occasional visit to that world would never be enough.

"Leslie?"

"Mmmm?"

He felt the soft fanning of her breath against his flesh and, impossibly, his body quickened. He clamped down on that sensation, concentrating instead on what he had to say. "Leslie"—now that he had decided to speak, he had trouble forming the words that would explain what he had learned about how he felt about her—"I'm sorry about today."

She came instantly awake, cocking her head back to look at him, searching his face in the moonlight but revealing nothing of what she thought in her expression. "Don't be," she said. Her lips turned up in a wistful, understanding smile. But she didn't understand, damn it! That much was evident when she spoke.

"I knew you were under a lot of pressure today." She lowered her head, not looking at him. "When Hank told me who Ken Johnson was, and when Hank let it slip— don't be angry with him, he thought I knew—that you were in the plane when it went down, I understood why. I—had expected you to shut me out."

Her words stunned him almost as much as the tone of her voice. Resigned. Accepting.

"You . . . expected me to shut you out?"

"You're a private person, David. Your grief is still very real to you. You told me from the first how much Elaine meant to you; how little anyone else could mean. That's one of the reasons why you agreed to our arrangement. I couldn't forget something that basic."

Arrangement. He didn't miss the subtle difference of the words. Arrangement. Not marriage. Between a woman who said she didn't believe in romantic love and a man who said he could never again feel it. Arrangement. Defined by legal terms to protect her child and nurture his.

She shifted in his arms and turned to look at him once again, concern and caring evident in her expression. She lifted her hand to his chest. "Are they so very bad, David?" she asked softly. "The memories?"

He lifted his hand to hers, trapping her healing touch against his cheek as he closed his eyes to the pain her question evoked. "God, yes," he said in a choked whisper.

"I'll listen if you want to talk," she told him. "Or I'll back away, change the subject, do *something,* if you don't want me to intrude."

The last thing he wanted to do was drag up the past; the past had its own horrible way of rearing up to remind him. But he had to; he was as aware of that fact as he was of the fragile woman in his arms. "Listen." He spoke so softly that he barely heard the word, but Leslie heard it. Nodding against his chest, she settled protectively against him.

"Hank—" He had to stop to clear the tightness in his throat. "Hank told you I was in the plane?" Again she nodded, a silent, waiting acceptance of his words. "What did you think when he told you?"

"I thought—" She hesitated as though searching for words. "I thought that even though your scars don't show, they must be horrendous. I thought . . . I thought that, more than once, you must have wondered why you didn't die, too."

"I did." He tightened his arms around her. Words jammed in his throat, in his mind, rivaling in intensity the visions they evoked, but, for the first time, David wanted to give them their freedom, wanted to know if, by releasing them, he could release himself.

"I didn't want to go on that trip," he told Leslie. "I'm never sick, but a virus had been working its way through the county and had latched onto me. Elaine had two horses entered in a race—one, a two-year-old filly that she had high hopes for. It meant so much to her, I couldn't stay home. At the race we ran into a friend, a medical doctor. Seeing what shape I was in, he badgered me until I gave in and took the antibiotics he pushed at me. When it came time to return home, I was in no shape to fly—I might not have been even without the antibiotics, but I'll never know now.

"Elaine was more than a competent pilot; I taught her to fly, and she had hundreds of hours logged. She was familiar with the plane; she was familiar with the terrain between the track and home. Tommy wanted to 'co-pilot'.

"I climbed into the backseat with Ellie, strapped myself in, and, shortly after takeoff, I went to sleep. I didn't wake up when Ellie unfastened her seatbelt and crawled over to my side of the seat. I didn't wake up until I heard Tommy cry out, and then it was too late. . . . The only thing I saw was Elaine's face, in profile, frozen in a silent scream, before we crashed into the trees. . . ." He paused, sucking in a deep, painful breath, willing himself to go on. To his own ears, his voice sounded strangely flat, afraid to convey the dangerous pain welling up within him.

"When I came to . . . Elaine and Tommy were dead. Ellie was crumpled on the floor at my feet. I was still strapped into my seat with no injuries other than a few bruised muscles, a few cuts from broken glass and tree branches."

He paused again, his breath coming quickly now, caught in the horror of that memory, then forced himself to continue. "Ellie was still alive—barely. I had a rough idea of where we were. I knew that if I waited for a rescue crew to find us, she might die, too. So I—so I rigged a makeshift carrier and walked out with her, leaving Elaine . . . and Tommy . . . alone on the mountain."

He felt moisture on his chest. Tears. Leslie's tears for him and all he had lost. Tears he'd never been able to shed for himself.

"I'll never know if I could have changed things—by staying awake, by insisting on sitting up front. I'll never know if I might have been able to take the controls, to avoid the crash."

"But you'll always wonder."

"Yes," he said. "I'll always wonder."

Leslie took a deep breath before placing her hand on his shoulder and gripping him. "Then wonder about this," she said with quiet intensity. "You saved your daughter's life. If you had been in the front, if you—" Her voice caught, then strengthened. "If you had been killed, too, what would have happened to her? Or Tommy, provided he hadn't been killed outright? Could either of them have survived without you?"

He pulled her to him, wrapping his arms around her, needing her warmth to drive out the chill that had overtaken him. He wanted to deny her words, but there was no way he could. "That's something else I'll never know."

She sighed against him, her breath warming him, her nearness warming him, holding him, just holding him, but giving him understanding, giving him comfort. Giving. As she never failed to do.

"Oh, Leslie," he murmured into her hair. "Don't let me hurt you."

He felt a small jolt of tension race through her before she spoke. "You won't," she promised. "You could never do that."

"Couldn't I?" It wasn't vanity that made him ask but concern. "I sometimes feel as though I've cheated you. You give so much; you need someone who's capable of giving in return."

She turned her face to his then. Her eyes were still bright with tears, her features tight with the effort of hiding her emotions. She shook her head, a small defiant movement. "You have given," she said in a voice as tight as her expression, "everything you promised to give. Mike is safe now, and I'll be forever grateful for that. As for anything else—"

Grateful. Leslie was grateful? He didn't want her gratitude. He didn't want to hear about it. He wanted to hear what he thought he'd seen in her until he drove her away from him. But her words went on, chilling him as quickly as she'd warmed him only a moment before.

"As for anything else, I won't ask for it, David. I don't expect it." Her voice seemed to break before she delivered the final blow. "I don't need it."

Chapter
10

THANK GOD SHE'D told David she didn't expect, didn't need, anything more from him than what he'd already given her, Leslie thought in a rare moment of bitterness, because in the almost six weeks since she'd made that brave but untrue statement, she certainly hadn't gotten more.

Not that he'd been unkind—Leslie doubted that David could be truly unkind to any living thing—just that he'd been absent. Busy preparing the ranch for winter. Busy with fall calving. Busy expanding a veterinarian practice that he had once deliberately limited. Busy, it seemed, with anything to keep him out of the house.

Too often, now, she was asleep before he came to bed, still asleep when he left her side before dawn. On those increasingly infrequent occasions when they came together in the night, in need, in longing, or in tender sharing, her love for him welled up within her, threatening to spill over in words he didn't want to hear. So, she thought, shaking off her gloom, maybe his absences were a mixed blessing. With him absent, no matter how much she missed him, she didn't have to maintain the facade of not loving him—a facade she knew she would continue to present until he gave some sign that he was ready for it to dissolve. Because having David, even without his love, was infinitely better than not having him at all.

He was busy tonight, this time on an errand for her, and as she glanced at the half-filled relish trays waiting on the long counter in front of her, she realized that she needed to get busy herself if she was going to have everything ready for the next day.

Her thoughts turned to the following day, to the surprise she had planned for Grace, to Grace herself and the gracious way she had welcomed Leslie into her family. Smiling, humming a persistent tune that had been running through her mind all day, she set to work.

She was still humming the tune, still working contentedly, when she became aware of David's presence, the delicious prickle of nerves along the back of her neck, the sensation of a lingering caress without physical touch, that always told her when he was near. She looked up to see him standing in the doorway, tired, as he almost always was these days, mud-spattered from the rain that had fallen steadily for the last two days, and—to her eyes, to the nerves that sensed him before she saw or heard him, to the longing awakening and twisting its way through her—devastatingly attractive.

"Hello," she said softly, betraying none of the turmoil within her.

He gave her a small smile, all the more endearing to her because of the weariness evident in his features, and walked across the den. Placing a couple of paper sacks to one side of her relish trays, he leaned back against the counter.

"Did you get Mike and Ellie delivered in time?"

He nodded. Without asking, she poured him a cup of coffee and handed it to him. He sipped gratefully before speaking. "According to Mike, there are some advantages to town living," he said, letting his smile flower into a grin. "I guess trick-or-treating and Halloween parties are part of them."

"I guess." Leslie turned back to her work, once again pretending, this time nonchalance. "Grace still has no idea?"

From the corner of her eye, she saw him shake his head. "No, but with as many people involved in this conspiracy of yours as there are, it's nothing short of a miracle that she doesn't. She'll be bringing the children home about noon tomorrow, and, as far as she knows, that's all she's doing—another favor for us."

Leslie abandoned her pretense of work. "She'll be pleased, won't she?" she asked hesitantly.

"Leslie." His voice softened, encouraging her. "She'll be ecstatic."

"Good," Leslie said, reassured, once again confident. "Birthdays are special." Remembering how late it was, she glanced up at him. "Are you hungry? I can fix you some supper."

He shook his head and stole a piece of cheese. "Go ahead with what you're doing," he said, surprisingly mellow, surprisingly relaxed. "I enjoy watching you fussing."

"Fussing?" Leslie put a little indignation in her teasing words; not much, because she didn't feel much. "Oh, David, don't let your mother hear you say that, or any of your cousins. They'll think you're a throwback to the dark ages." Smiling, happy beyond all reason at the closeness she felt with him, she added, "And I won't let them know how much I enjoy doing just that."

She glanced at a large sack on the counter. "What is that? Another present for your mother?"

"Nope," he said slowly. "Why don't you take a look inside?"

Her curiosity heightened by his air of secrecy, Leslie pulled out the large, flat box and opened it. "Boots?" she asked, looking at the soft brown leather, the delicate, intricately stitched pattern of the tops.

"You've needed some for a long time, but you have such a tiny foot I had trouble finding what I wanted for you. That's why it took so long."

"For me?" she whispered. Hesitantly she reached to touch the leather as she felt her eyes misting. David had given her so much, his home, his family, his name, but he had never *given* her anything before. "They're beautiful." Hurriedly, she carried them over to the kitchen stool and shucked off her tennis shoes. There were boot socks in the box, too, thoughtfully provided by him. She pulled on a pair of the socks and tugged on the boots. She stood up, grinning, as she stamped her feet further into the comfortable snugness and took a few steps. "And a perfect fit."

"They'd better be," he said, laughing, openly sharing her enthusiasm. "I borrowed a pair of your shoes for the bootmaker to use as a pattern."

The gift had seemed perfect before, but knowing that it wasn't just something he'd picked up on a whim but something he'd carefully designed made it even more so. "They're wonderful," she said softly. Surely it would be all right to touch him, to hug him. A show of appreciation for his thoughtfulness. That was all it had to seem. She went to him, as she had wanted to from the moment he'd entered the room, slid her arms around him, and rested her head on his chest. "Thank you."

"Now I won't have to worry about you wandering

around in the woods with no more protection than those
tennis shoes," he said, dismissing her words but sliding
his arms around her, holding her loosely to his chest,
"or getting a foot caught in the stirrup." His hands
splayed across her back, bringing her closer to him.
"Or..."

All thought of gratitude, appreciation, or pretense
fled as David lifted her to him, bent his head and covered her mouth with his, seeking, then demanding, a
response from her—a response, if he but knew it, that
was his without asking. Leslie surrendered to the need
claiming her, to the matching need she felt in David,
holding him to her, never wanting to let him go, as she
matched the aggressive plunder of his mouth, as she
treasured each point of contact between them—not
enough, never enough.

She felt him pulling away and opened her eyes, questioning him silently.

"The telephone," he said on a ragged breath.

Only then did she hear the shrill intrusion. She
sagged against him, legs too weak to carry her. "It's
probably Susan," she told him, her voice as ragged as
his. "She and Ben are coordinating the invitations and
who's bringing what out from town." She knew she
ought to answer the summons but couldn't find the
strength to leave David's arms. "Or Mabel. She's feeling better. She swears it's just a bout of chronic bron-
chitis. Her granddaughter Meg called while I was over
there this afternoon. She's coming to stay with them for
a while." Leslie knew she was babbling, but she
couldn't help herself. She had the insane feeling that
once she walked away from him, once she answered the
telephone, everything between them would be changed.

The phone shrieked again. David drew a deep breath
and stepped away from her. "Do you want me to get it?"

"No." Surprisingly, her legs supported her. She
raised her head and sighed. "No. It's probably for me."

There was so much she wanted to say to him, so much she couldn't say. "I'm sorry."

He smiled ruefully at her and lifted his hand to her cheek. "Me, too."

Why now? Leslie thought as she belatedly hurried to snatch up the receiver. Her voice, still husky with emotion, managed only one word, a shaky "hello," before she recognized the voice on the other end of the line and her carefully constructed pretend world came crashing down around her. She grabbed the wall for support as she felt her strength draining from her.

"Leslie," Leta Burgess said in her beautifully modulated voice, not bothering to mask her disdainful amusement. "Did you really think you could hide from us?"

David drove. Leslie was incapable of doing so, even if he'd been willing to let her, which he wasn't. And he'd be damned before he'd invite those people out to his home without meeting them first, without seeing for himself the person who could, with only a few words, change the laughing, secure woman he knew into the pale shadow who now huddled silently on the opposite end of the truck seat.

Leslie had said little since he took the telephone receiver from her, only listening to him as he made the arrangements with Leta Burgess and agreeing numbly to meet with them at an all-night cafe about halfway between their home and the town where the Burgesses were staying. Leslie had wanted to change clothes, to dress for her meeting with her former in-laws, but David had stopped her. To him, she was beautiful, no matter what she wore. Now he wondered, perhaps he should have let her change, if the armor of something other than snugly fitting jeans and a loose, casually styled sweater would have helped sustain her.

When they reached the restaurant, David helped Leslie from the truck. She visibly straightened, steeling her spine and squaring her shoulders, but didn't speak. The inside of the cafe was crowded, filled with truckers, cowboys, and neighbors, many of whom called out friendly greetings to him and Leslie, but he had no trouble recognizing Harrison and Leta Burgess. They sat in a booth in the back of the room, isolated by distance, by dress, and by their attitude of condescending superiority.

David fielded the comments from his neighbors, but his attention was devoted to Leslie as they worked their way toward the back booth. With his hand at the small of her back, guiding her, he felt the small tremors that worked through her. Leslie was terrified of the woman, he was sure of that, although he didn't yet understand why. But he was equally sure that she would never show her fear.

David let Leslie slide into the booth before seating himself on the outside and draping an arm over the back of the booth to rest his hand on her shoulder. Leta cast one quick, disdainful glance over his worn work clothes; Harrison's eyes lingered a little longer, speculative but seeing nothing but outward appearances.

"This is your . . . husband?" Leta acknowledged him and dismissed him in those four words.

Leslie's head shot up, her small chin jutted out, and her eyes flashed. "Yes."

The waitress approached with a coffee pot. Harrison waved her away, but David called her back. "Leslie and I would like some of that, Hazel." He slowed his voice, exaggerating the drawl Leslie had once teased him about. He upended two of the coffee cups and glanced at the grim couple across the table. "You folks sure you don't want some?"

Leta grimaced; Harrison shook his head. David smiled up at the waitress. "How's your milk cow coming along?" Hazel's cow had rot foot, a fairly serious but not uncommon ailment, one that was reasonably easy to treat. With a few questions of Hazel, David elicited most of the unpleasant details from her while he studied the Burgesses without seeming to. He'd met people like them before, on the racing circuit. It was one of the things he liked least about racing, the people —not many, but enough so that he'd learned to recognize them—who were beautiful on the outside but devoid of any human warmth, any consideration for anything but their own selfishness.

Leta was the perpetrator in this scene. He recognized that immediately. Leslie had told him that Harrison was a banker. He imagined Harrison acted quite differently in the board room, but in matters of family, he had delegated his responsibility to his wife, probably years before, and she had taken that responsibility and run with it.

"I see no point in wasting time," Leta said the moment Hazel left the table. "We've come for Mike."

"No." Leslie's soft word hung in the silence at the table. David wondered if he was the only one who heard the determination, the strength behind it.

"Leslie." Leta's determination was more apparent. "This charade has gone on long enough. Don't force us to take legal action against you. Don't force us to drag Mike through a court battle you can't hope to win."

David squeezed Leslie's shoulder, reminding her that he was with her, but he remained silent.

"You are the one who is forcing the issue, Leta, not me. I never wanted to deprive you of Mike. I still don't. You are his grandparents. He needs to know you. He needs to be able to visit with you. But I am his mother. I will not tolerate your threats any longer. And you will not take my son away from me."

Leta leaned back in the booth, studying Leslie. "You've grown claws," she said finally. "I suppose this . . . farmer you've married has given you some sort of false courage."

David ignored the insult. Whoever had provided the Burgesses with their information on Leslie's whereabouts had obviously been less than thorough, and, right now, that was fine with him.

"But false courage won't help. This sham of a marriage won't help; not when we expose it for what it is, a deliberate attempt to delude the court. How did you find *him?* Never mind. I really don't care. Breeding will always show, Leslie. You've sold yourself again. This time for considerably less than when you married Michael."

Leslie had paled. With each of Leta's words, she grew increasingly more pale. David watched silently as long as he could. "That's enough," he said, interrupting Leta's attack.

"This is none of your business," Leta said coldly.

"You're wrong," he told her, abandoning his exaggerated drawl and speaking with deadly calm. "It's very much my business. Leslie is my wife. Adoption proceedings are already underway; in a few months, Mike will be my son. And you're right. Breeding does show." He ought to stop; he had never criticized Leslie's marriage before, knowing she had heard enough criticism without having to listen to his, but he could no longer keep silent. "What kind of breeding produces a grown man, a senior medical student, capable of seducing a fifteen-year-old child who is still suffering the shock of losing her mother to a terminal illness?" He paused for only a second, not expecting an answer. "Obviously the same kind of breeding that produces people who can stand back and watch while their grandchild's parent faces poverty, gloating because she's no longer able to protect herself. Thank God, I don't see that kind of breeding in Mike. Leslie's done a fine job of raising him, without any help. She's imbued him with honor, caring, integrity—qualities that had to come from somewhere, and I damn sure don't see them in you."

David couldn't ever remember being so angry, but he kept his voice tightly checked. Leslie was strong, but he no longer wondered why she had come to him exhausted. What he did wonder was how, after years of fending off their ridicule and their threats, had she kept from breaking long ago?

He snatched a napkin from the holder and a pen from his pocket, sketched a brief map and handed it to Harrison Burgess, not trusting himself to speak to Leta. "If you want to see Mike, come to our home tomorrow afternoon. Don't come before two; I won't let you on the property. Don't come at all unless you can show Leslie the respect she deserves."

Standing, he held his hand out for Leslie. She took it, drawing on his strength as he helped her from the booth, but once on her feet she stood straight and as tall as her diminutive height would let her. David put his arm around her waist, sensing she would welcome his support even if she wouldn't ask for it, even if she gave no outward sign of needing it. He glanced back at Harrison. "And don't come with the intention of discussing any of this with Mike."

In the truck on the way home, Leslie sat rigidly upright on the seat, still silent. David glanced at her frequently, measuring her reaction, weighing her silence.

Pride, strength, courage, and loyalty—Leslie had all those things, a tough combination wrapped up in a fragile package that was never meant to be tough. David reached for her, brushing the hair back from her cheek with a gentle touch. Leslie jumped slightly and turned her head toward him, giving him another glimpse of her ashen complexion, her haunted eyes. And before him— David remembered things she had told him, understood things she had left unsaid—before him, Leslie had never had anyone she could depend upon, anyone she could lean on.

He wanted her to depend upon him, he wanted to share his strength with her, he wanted to give her some of the comfort she had given him during the time she'd been with him. He pulled his truck to the shoulder of the road and parked. Turning, he reached for her. "Come here," he coaxed.

She hesitated, then with a rush she was in his arms, her arms around him, holding him fiercely, while tremors shook her. "Did you mean it?" she whispered against his chest. "What you said to them?"

"All of it," he told her, raising a hand to smooth the hair from her face. She felt so right in his arms. So right. "And more."

The next day dawned bright and clear, without a hint of the previous day's rain. The brisk breeze, not yet cool enough to justify a woodfire in any of the fireplaces, carried the promise of autumn, and the mountains blazed with the glory of fall foliage. Leslie stood in the open doorway of her bedroom, looking out over the deck, over the bright blue cover of the swimming pool, over the palette of colors spread across a rugged landscape that had once intimidated her, loathe to leave the room where, throughout the night, for the first time in her life, she had felt . . . cherished.

The memory of last night should be bringing her nothing but quiet joy and hope for her future with David, she told herself as she leaned against the door facing, letting the cool breeze play over her. Instead, it filled her with vague longings, a sense of loss, and a quiet, desperate anger that she tried to fight. Not anger at David, but at—herself?—fate, circumstances, whatever it was that had caused her to live as long as she had without ever having known that feeling before. And anger at Leta, and yes, this time at herself. David was right. When she had finally begun to listen to him, she had realized how right he was. Once the very real threat of a custody suit was removed, Leta had no power over her other than what Leslie gave her. But, God, she had given her power. And why? For acceptance, perhaps, starting when Leslie had been a frightened fifteen-year-old. Well, she was no longer frightened, she was no longer fifteen, and she no longer needed acceptance from a woman whose values were so different from her own.

And David was right about something else. Neither one of them really needed the protection of his family the next time they faced Harrison and Leta, but the Burgesses understood two weapons: power and wealth. Bringing them to the house during Grace's birthday party would demonstrate wordlessly that they were at least equally matched in those areas, and far outdistanced by something even more important: a united, caring front.

Grace arrived at noon, as arranged, bringing Mike and Ellie home. Leslie met them at the front door as they piled out of the car, talking excitedly about something—not the party, because Mike and Ellie didn't know about that. She smiled at the picture her son had made. For someone who hadn't wanted to become a cowboy, he was doing his best to look like one: worn, faded jeans, a western shirt half pulled from the waistband, a battered hat, and boots, already scuffed and well used.

She had to tell him. Quickly. Before she lost her nerve. "Hi, there," she said. "Did you have a good time?"

Ellie ran to her for a hug, but Mike just held up a bulging paper bag. "Great. Popcorn balls. Candy." His grin changed to grimace. "Fruit."

Leslie chuckled and kept her voice light. "You two need to get cleaned up for lunch."

"Oh, Mom," Mike asked. "Do we have to? Now?"

"Now." And yes, Leslie, she thought, knowing she could put it off no longer, *now.* "Mike—your grandparents will be here this afternoon."

Mike looked at her in stunned surprise. Then his face split in a wide smile. "You told them." He ran to her, hugging her tightly. "Oh, Mom. Thanks."

Leslie looked over his head at Grace, waiting silently.

"Come on, kid," Mike said, breaking away from her and turning to Ellie. "Race you upstairs."

Leslie didn't reprimand him, didn't try to stop them as they ran into the house, just stood there trying to tell herself that her son's enthusiasm was a natural reaction, nothing more.

"You didn't tell them, did you?"

Leslie sighed and turned to Grace. "No."

Grace walked to her and enfolded her in a loose hug. "Do you want me to stick around? I've had a few lessons in social intimidation in my day."

Leslie could only shake her head and smile weakly. How had she ever compared Grace with Leta? Even with surface similarities, there was a wealth of difference—obvious, real difference—between the two women. With regret that Grace's birthday celebration would be interrupted, Leslie slipped her arm around the other woman's waist. "Of course I want you to stick around," she said as they walked together into the house, "but not because of them."

When Phil arrived with Angela, Grace was surprised and pleased. When Ben and Susan and their children came in a few minutes later, she looked suspiciously at David. But when Eunice and her four boys swooped in, Leslie saw no sense in trying to hide what was already obvious. She opened the door to the den and moved the party into that room, where tables had already been set up and an enormous cake waited. For the second time that day, Grace, her eyes moist but her face wreathed in a satisfied smile, hugged Leslie.

By two o'clock the entire clan had gathered, noisily, companionably, spilling out from the huge den into the pool area. Leslie wiped damp palms on her jeans and cast frequent, furtive glances at the door. She no longer had anything to fear from Leta, she knew that, but it seemed that *knowing* and *feeling* were two different things.

She saw them the moment they entered the room, pausing, glancing over the room, trying to hide their surprise at the house and the crowd. Harrison was being more successful than Leta.

Mike saw them, calling out "Grandma!" in a loud voice, and Leslie saw Leta wince at the familiar term that Grace encouraged.

With her eyes she sought out David, finding him across the room. Their gazes met, locked. In complete understanding they began walking toward the door, arriving, together, only seconds after Mike. Leta knelt before Mike, grabbing him in possessive arms. For a moment Mike surrendered to her, then his welcoming smile faded and he began struggling against what Leslie knew he felt as an unseemly public display of affection. Reluctantly, Leta loosened her hold on him, gazing at him with what looked like love, with what looked like adoration.

Mike squirmed once more in the loose embrace, then held out his hand and dragged his ever-present shadow toward him. Still flushed with excitement, he turned to his grandparents. "I want you to meet someone. Ellie, this is my grandma and grandpa from New Jersey." He tugged Ellie even closer. "This is my new sister," he said with obvious pride. "She doesn't play with dolls or anything, but she's okay. She can fight almost as good as a boy."

Leslie winced. There were so many good things

Mike could have said about Ellie; why had he picked that one? She felt a huge hand drop onto her shoulder and looked up. Phil stood behind her; Ben, only a foot or so from David; Grace, between the two of them.

Leta barely spared a glance for Ellie, but Leslie saw her as Leta must have. For the first time in years, if she didn't count the day of the fight, Ellie looked less than perfect. Her braid had come undone; she had a smudge of dirt across her cheek.

"*This* is how you're raising Michael's son?"

Leslie met Leta's angry glare with a steady gaze of her own. Yes, she was still afraid of Leta, but it wasn't the mindless fear that had gripped her for so many years. "This is part of what *my* son is learning," she said evenly.

"I won't have it. Mike, get your things, we're taking you home."

"Burgess," David warned quietly.

It was Mike who broke the silence. "But I am home," he said.

"Home is with us. In New Jersey. Leslie had no right to bring you here."

"Leta, stop this," Leslie began. "Don't ruin what chance we have left to be a family—," but Mike interrupted her, turning in confusion to look at her.

"What about Mom?" he asked.

"Your mother made her decision when she came here. She had no right to steal you from us, to hide you from us. She obviously didn't care for our feelings—"

"But she made me write you every week."

Leslie wanted to reach out to him, to touch him, to hold him, but he stood defiantly proud.

"Writing isn't the same as seeing," Leta said. "No court in the land will keep you from us."

"You haven't a prayer," Ben said softly, but his words were almost lost in Mike's angry denial. Whirling, Mike ran from the room. Leslie turned to follow him, but Phil's hand on her shoulder stopped her. Phil was right, of course. Mike was surrounded by family, just as she was.

Rising to her feet, Leta turned to Ben with chilling disdain. "You're an expert, I presume."

"You might say so." Ben's voice softened into the country casualness that hid a sharp wit and even sharper knowledge of the law. "Since Mike's adoption is already underway, the court you're going to have to convince is the one down here." He gave Leslie a little smile before his features settled into deceptive blandness. "I hope I have enough professional integrity to disqualify myself, but I probably don't, so it looks like I'm the judge you're going to have to persuade that Leslie, a woman I've often entrusted with my own children, is not fit to raise her own."

Leta opened her mouth to speak, but before she could, Harrison did. "Leta," he said with quiet authority. "One thing you learn in business is when to recognize a loss." He glanced from Leslie to David, and for a moment Leslie saw more than the quiet man who had always stood back and let Leta speak. "We've been out-maneuvered."

Leslie didn't relax until she saw the Burgesses' rental car disappear out of sight on its way down their long drive. She turned to David, standing in the doorway beside her. He pulled her to him in a sustaining hug. "Are you all right?" he asked.

"Yes." She smiled up at him. "Yes." For the first time in years, maybe ever. In his arms she was more than all right.

She wasn't all right a few minutes later when she tried to find Mike. He wasn't in the house; he wasn't out by the pool.

"He left," Ben, Jr. finally told her, "while you and Dad were talking with those other people."

She turned to David, clutching his arm. "No," he said, acknowledging her fears and calming them with uncanny perception. "There's no way he went with them. Not after today."

"Ellie followed him," Angela volunteered. "I'm sorry, Leslie. I didn't see any reason to stop them."

"It's all right, Angela," Leslie said, turning to David, pleading with him silently to tell her that it was, truly all right. "They have to be around here somewhere."

They weren't at the Bakers' house. A quick telephone call confirmed that, and a few minutes later Hank joined a search of the barns. They weren't there either, and neither was the jeep. Jake remembered seeing the jeep headed south, into the mountains.

"Mike can't drive," Leslie whispered.

"Uh—" It was one of Eunice's twins. "Yes, he can. The night of the campout, he wanted to learn. I—uh—I gave him a lesson."

"Oh, my God." One lesson, weeks before, and Mike and Ellie were out in rough, wild land in a vehicle that required both skill and strength.

David caught her arms in his hands and forced her to look at him. His eyes mirrored her own fears, but he held her still. "They can't have gone far," he told her. "We'll find them."

Chapter

11

HOURS! LESLIE PACED the den restlessly, impatiently. It seemed like hours since the men and older boys had left, taking every four-wheel-drive vehicle on the place and fanning out in a wide pattern to search the ranch roads and logging trails to the south, while the women had closed ranks, tightening into a protective circle around her. She cast an anxious glance outside, knowing that her worry had made the time seem longer than it had been. But how much time did they have left until dark, until they had to call in the sheriff and an organized search, until she knew *something?*

"Leslie." Ben, Jr. spoke to her hesitantly. Eleven, only a little younger than Mike, he thought he should have been allowed to go with the search party, had resented being left behind, and since that time had been unusually silent.

"Leslie," he said again, this time more insistently. "I—I think I know where they went."

Leslie stopped her pacing and turned to him, grabbing his shoulders. "Where?"

"We aren't—I mean, I promised, we all did, that we wouldn't say anything about them—"

"For God's sake, Ben," Susan said, bending to her son. "I know promises are important, but Mike and Ellie could be in danger."

"The caves," he said. "I took him down there when we camped out, you know, let him in on the secret, told him about outlaws hiding out there."

"Of course." Susan hugged her son and turned to Leslie. "We should have thought of them."

"You know about the caves?" Ben asked.

Susan smiled at him and shook her head. "Your father's known about them since he was your age and thought his folks didn't know where they were, either." Her smile faded. "But they're to the north, not the south."

Outlaw caves. They would have fascinated Mike, and Leslie knew he was bright enough to leave a false trail—if he wasn't simply rushing away in a blind panic. "Where are they?"

"There's an old homesite—Ben's grandmother was born there—"

"I know the place," Leslie told her. Thanks to David's sharing it with her.

"Good. There's a ledge below it, and then another drop off. The caves are in that ledge."

Leslie placed a consoling hand on young Ben's shoulder. "Thank you." Then, turning, she ran from the room.

* * *

No vehicle remaining at the house could climb the steep, narrow trails leading to the homesite, but Henry could, and—thanks to the bareback pad Hank had given her—he had done so more than once in the past six weeks. He knew the trail almost as well as Leslie, but not at the pace she now took it, digging the heels of her new boots into his flanks and urging him onward.

She found the jeep at the last bend in the navigable trail, wedged between a young tree and a large rock. Sobbing in exhaustion and relief, she slid from Henry's back. The jeep was stuck, not wrecked. She struggled up the remaining short distance, pausing at the top to call Mike's name, then Ellie's, but receiving no answer.

In all the times she'd been there, she had never explored the sloping ledge. She approached it reluctantly, but, if generations of boys had crawled all over it, nothing could keep her from doing the same, from finding her children. She eased herself over the edge, feeling the loose rock sliding beneath the still slick, new leather soles of her boots, grabbing for handholds and toeholds until she stood at last on solid ground.

"Mike!" she called out. "Ellie!" Still receiving no answer, she took a deep, quavering breath and began carefully picking her way along what seemed to be a narrow path.

She found Mike sitting in the mouth of a cave, sullen and silent as he watched her approach, with Ellie beside him, just as silent, tear tracks marking her dusty face.

"I'm not going with them," he said when at last she stood in front of him. "They can't make me."

"Oh, honey." Leslie dropped to her knees before him. "No one is even going to try." She reached for the two of them, feeling tears on her own cheeks. "We're home now. All of us. And this is where we're going to stay."

* * *

They couldn't get out. After such a tearful, and joy-
ful, reunion, it seemed so anticlimactic—stupid even—
but, Leslie thought, undeniably true. None of them was
quite tall enough to reach the first secure footing.

"How did you and Ben get out?" Leslie asked after
several futile attempts.

"It didn't seem so far," Mike said. "I think something's broke loose."

"Oh, great." Leslie stood back and studied the problem. "What if I boost you?" she asked. "Then I can lift
Ellie up to you, and you can reach down and help me."

"I'll boost you," Mike said with a stubborn male
pride that brought a smile to Leslie's face.

She shook her head. "Sorry, but one of us may have
to be pulled out of here, and I just don't think I can lift
you that far, Mike."

Even Mike had to agree with the logic of that, and
although reluctant to be the first out, he stepped into her
locked hands and vaulted lightly upward. Something
probably had broken loose, Leslie thought, because it
was still breaking loose, small rock and grit sliding beneath her feet, making her balance precarious, but she
took Ellie, guiding her upward and pushing on her small
back until Mike grabbed the little girl and pulled her to
safety, too.

"Come on, Mom." Mike bent over the ledge, holding
his hands out for her. "You're going to have to jump."
Leslie jumped, missing his outstretched fingers by
inches, sliding on the rock beneath her feet. She bal-
anced herself, concentrated on what she had to do, and
tried again. This time she actually touched his fingertips
before falling back, but this time she didn't regain her
balance. She came down hard, rock shifting beneath
her, and landed in a sliding sprawl.

"Are you all right?" Mike yelled frantically.

"I think so," Leslie called back shakily, but when she

tried to stand, she knew she wasn't. A sharp jolt of pain speared her left ankle. "Oh, great," she muttered. "Of all the stupid—" It was either sprained or broken, she didn't know which, but either one was bad enough. There was no way she could climb out.

"I'm coming down for you."

"Don't be silly," she almost screamed. She fought to control her voice. She mustn't panic the children. "Then we'd all be trapped here. Go for help."

"I can't leave you here!"

"You have to. Take Ellie to the house and bring David back. Please, Mike." And when it looked as though pleading wouldn't help, she ordered him. "Now."

She lowered herself carefully to the rock, bracing herself with widespread hands as she listened to the children's voices fading into the distance. Thank God, both of them could ride. Thank God, she had brought Henry instead of trying to drive.

She drew another shaky breath and looked around her. What was she, a city girl, doing, sitting here all alone on a rocky mountain slope? But she wasn't a city girl any longer, Leslie realized. And she wasn't alone. She learned that when she lifted her arm to wipe dust and grit from her face, displacing more gravel, which slithered and bounced down the slope. She followed the sound idly, waiting for it to stop. It didn't. If anything it grew louder, a dry, persistent rattling that lasted long after the rock should have fallen over the edge. Leslie glanced downward. On a flat rock far below her, but not far enough for comfort, curled a large, brown snake. It had been sunning itself probably, before being angered by the falling rock. Now it had its head up, its tail stiffly erect, and it was that tail that was making all the noise.

Her heart thudded, sending the blood pounding through her temples, and she felt the suddenly chill breeze on her overheated face. *They won't go out of their way to attack,* she heard David saying as he had that night long ago, as clearly as though he were right beside her.

"That's all right, fellow," she whispered silently to the snake, "neither will I. And just as soon as David gets here, you can have your home all to yourself again."

She knew it would be David who came for her. Not Phil or Ben or even Hank. Not after last night. And she knew also that he would be furious with her for acting so rashly, for not finding him to let him go to the rescue.

Her ankle was aching now, but not too badly. Maybe it was just sprained after all; but even with a sprain it would soon start swelling. Swelling? Leslie realized what that could mean, and swore at herself again for her stupidity. Unless she did something soon, they would have to cut her boot off her foot, her beautiful new boot that David had given her only the night before. "Not in this lifetime," she muttered, bending and carefully tugging until she freed her foot. Grinning, pleased with her foresight and her success, she turned to place the boot on a flat, safe place only a few feet away, stretching as she did so.

She was still grinning when she started to slide. She threw her hands out to stop herself, felt the abrasion of small stones beneath her palms, but kept on sliding, then tumbling, rolling down the slope, toward the flat rock and the sunning rattlesnake. Her mouth opened in a scream that never sounded. She glimpsed the snake as she rolled into him, felt a sharp, hot pain in her leg, and then she and the snake were careening out of control, toward the edge, toward a fall that neither one of them could survive.

"No," she prayed silently, twisting her body, scrambling for some kind of handhold. "Not now. Please."

She hit a boulder near the edge with enough force to knock what little breath she had left out of her. She lay there dazed, listening to stones, gravel, and rock, falling away beneath her, bouncing over other rocks on their way down. Cautiously she raised her head. The snake was nowhere to be seen. Her left foot lay only inches from the edge.

Oh, David, she thought, swallowing convulsively, *I'm in a real mess now.*

She bent her knee, inching her leg up to confirm what she already knew. Two angry red punctures marred the outside of her calf just above the sock.

What do you do if you're bitten by a snake? she heard the familiar ritual the children had been forced to go through time after time. *Sit down. Send someone for help. Don't panic!*

What do you do if you're alone and bitten by a snake? Walk, don't run to the house. Don't panic!

Well, Mike and Ellie had gone for help, but not for a snake bite. And she couldn't walk anywhere. The only thing she could do was not panic. She felt hysterical laughter welling within her. *Don't panic.*

There was a snakebite kit in the first aid box in the jeep. All the ranch vehicles carried them. But it might as well be a hundred miles from here. What was in it? She tried to think. Anti-venom. Adrenalin. A vicious little razor to cut open the wound. Forget that. She had nothing to use. A suction device. Forget that, too. She couldn't even reach the wound. A tourniquet.

Leslie lay back cautiously. She had that—if she could work her belt loose. Her leg already felt as if it were on fire; it was already swelling, growing heavy. She wasn't going to panic. And she wasn't going to die. Not when she had so much to live for. She felt a damp chill as the breeze picked up, and she looked defiantly at the darkening sky. David would get there in time. He had to. Not just for her sake—but for his. He might not love her, but he did care for her. And he musn't be forced to go through losing another wife, especially not in the mountains that he loved so much.

The sky was totally dark when Leslie heard the shouts from the top of the ledge and saw beams of light searching the rock. She opened her mouth to call out but all that emerged was a hoarse croak, not loud enough to carry more than a few feet. Sometime during her wait, she couldn't remember when, she had closed her fist over a large rock. She lifted it, recognizing but not understanding why it took all her strength, and hit it against the boulder that was supporting her, over and over and over, a pitiful, rhythmic tapping, stopping only when she heard David's voice, hoarse from yelling, call out, "Down there," and then felt herself spotlighted in a flashlight's beam.

She dropped her arm to her side and waited as the light approached, too fast, she thought, wanting to warn him, too fast; you'll fall. But before she could find the words, David dropped to his knees beside her, his face lighted by the flashlight he placed near her head, tight with strain, grim, softening as he reached out his trembling hands to touch her.

She saw him swallow once, a quick convulsive movement. "How's the other fellow?" he asked softly.

She could still smile. At least the muscles in her face worked. "I think I killed him," she whispered through a mouth that felt full of cotton.

He shook his head. "You look like you tangled with a bear."

"Just a snake."

His hand froze against her cheek. His body tightened. "You weren't bitten?"

"I'm afraid so."

He closed his eyes, bending his head away from her, then his arms tightened around her, lifting her. She felt so light in his arms. How could that be, when her leg was so, so heavy? And then Leslie knew. David hadn't gotten there in time after all.

She lifted her hand to touch his cheek and watched her fingers float through the air. "David? I have to tell you something."

"Now, Leslie? Can't it wait? I need to get you out of here."

No. It wouldn't wait. His face was beautiful in the reflected glow of the flashlight, almost otherworldly, as it swam before her eyes. She brushed her fingers over his cheek, thought for a moment she could feel moisture beneath her touch, and then her world spun crazily around her. "I—" She forced her eyes to remain open, forced her voice to obey her. "I love you."

Installed on the comfortable sofa in her bedroom, a cheerful fire blazing in the fireplace, Leslie leaned back and surveyed her leg propped up on pillows. A brown elastic bandage wrapped her ankle, which was broken, although not too badly. Which was fortunate, she admitted to herself, because the white surgical gauze and tape covering the snakebite wound precluded any plaster cast, at least for a while. "Colorful," she muttered, casting a last disparaging glance at her battle scars and assorted bruises. But it wasn't battle scars she wanted to think about. At least not those that showed.

David had been with her when she first woke up in Fort Smith Hospital, had been with her even before that in a memory that was so nebulous it seemed like a dream. Perhaps it had been. She'd been surrounded in the dark by a swarm of bees. She couldn't see them; she could only hear them. Droning. Endlessly. As she struggled in the arms of a big red bear. Phil's voice, disembodied, saying, "She's conscious." David's voice, so low, so hoarse she barely recognized it. "We're almost there. The ambulance is already waiting at the airport."

Only it wasn't a dream. Leslie knew that now. After

two years, David had flown. For her. She wanted to cry for the painful effort it must have cost him to do that. But he hadn't spoken of it in the two days he stayed with her at the hospital. And he hadn't spoken of something else: those last words she remembered just before she lost consciousness; the words she had thought she would never have another chance to say.

And in the hours since he'd carried her into the house and settled her on the couch, he had not once been back in the room.

Everyone else had been to see her; more than once. Hank with firewood. Mabel with homemade soup. Grace with hot tea. The children, separately and together. Doing for her. All of them. Showing her wordlessly how much they cared for her.

She heard the click of the door shutting, the separate click of the lock, and looked up to see David leaning back against the door. "I'm sorry," he said. "It's the only way we can have any privacy. I almost had to take a number to get in here." He stood there hesitantly, questioningly. "How do you feel?"

Awful, she thought, *frightened, lonely. I want you beside me, David, holding me*. She couldn't say that; she'd said too much already. But she could answer him with another truthful statement. "Pampered." To her dismay she felt tears overflowing, running unchecked down her cheeks. She gestured toward the fire, a nearby tray, a stack of books. "I—I've never had anyone do so much for me before."

Silently he walked to her and sat beside her on the sofa, reaching out with a gentle hand to touch her tears. "Then it's time someone did," he said softly.

He was close, so close. Leslie could no longer resist. She leaned forward, resting her head on his chest and sliding her arms around his waist. She loved him, loved the strength in his well-honed body, loved the tenderness that was as much a part of him as his strength.

"You flew me to the hospital," she said against his chest. "I'm sorry you had to do that. Thank you."

His arms tightened around her, and his words echoed through her, clipped and tense. "I don't want your thanks, Leslie."

Stunned, she tried to pull away from him, but he wouldn't let her. Holding her head against him as his fingers tangled in her hair, he went on in the same clipped voice. "Do you remember what you said to me on the mountain?"

This was it, then. The moment she had been dreading and longing for. "Yes."

"Did you mean it?" he asked. "Or did you say it because you thought it was what I wanted to hear?"

She could lie to him, pretend that she'd been delirious with pain. Maybe he would believe her. Maybe they could go back to what they'd had before. No. She'd had to break her leg, fall off a mountain, be bitten by a rattlesnake, and think she was dying before she had found the courage to say those words, but she wouldn't deny them. Not now. And she couldn't lie to him, Leslie realized, not ever again. No matter what the consequences.

"David," she said, tired, resigned, and for once not trying to hide that, either, "only in my dreams have I ever thought you wanted to hear me say I love you. I said it because I could no longer *not* say it."

She felt a shudder run through him before he bent his head to hers. "Leslie, Leslie," he murmured as his lips brushed against her throat, her cheek, her eyelids. "I've wanted to hear it for so long, I was afraid—. You do that, you know, give other people what they need, what they want. I wanted to ask you the moment you woke up, but I couldn't face learning that this was just another act of giving."

"David." Wonder filled her. She moved in his embrace, twisting her head to look at him. He captured her mouth, plundering it, a hungry man, starving for her, but he was no hungrier than she. His hands roamed restlessly but gently over her; hers worked their way up, around his neck, to capture his head and hold him even closer to her, while she met his hunger, answered it, found the honeyed sweetness of his mouth—yes, giving, but this time taking, too. Taking for all the times she had held back, for all the times she had pretended, for all the times she had wanted to be in his arms in just this way.

He eased her against the pillows, tenderly following her down, his chest a treasured and tantalizing weight against her breasts, his arms a welcome haven, his mouth—his mouth a glimpse of heaven. Leslie moaned his name, twisting against him.

He pulled away from her, slowly, reluctantly, and held her face cradled in his hands as he looked wonderingly into her eyes. "I fought loving you," he said, "longer and harder than any sane man would have, and with no reason now that even makes sense to me. And when I finally realized that I didn't have to fight you, that you were all that I'd ever want, more than I'd ever need, I thought I had driven you away from me." His eyes darkened; his face clouded over. "You . . . pulled away from me. You . . ."

Leslie knew all too well what his stammered words meant, remembered all too well the effort it had taken to do what he was accusing her of. "Hiding how much I loved you," she whispered. "Because I didn't think you wanted my love. I wasn't sure you wanted me."

"I want it," he groaned, pulling her once again into his arms. "I want you. I need you, Leslie, like I have never needed another person. But I didn't know I loved you; I didn't know I was capable of loving you until—" Another shudder wracked him. "And then—God, when I thought I'd lost you, I—"

She caught his face in her hands, silencing him with

her mouth, soothing him with her touch, until touch became more than soothing, became demanding. Once again, he pulled away from her. "You'll stay with me then? You'll be my wife?"

"Oh, David," her voice broke on a sobbing chuckle, "I *am* your wife."

He looked down at her, his eyes full of the love she had longed to see there. "Yes," he said softly. "Yes, you are."

He traced his fingers down her cheek to the hollow of her throat. "But we have to do something to celebrate this," he said, and Leslie knew that by "this" he meant their new-found love, wonderful, glorious love, and a new beginning for both of them.

"We'll have another ceremony," he said. "We'll have Ben come out to the house, invite the family—"

"No," she said, smiling weakly, "I don't need that."

"A honeymoon. We never did have one."

"David," she said gently, loving him even more. "No, I don't need that, either."

"Then we'll tear up that damned agreement."

She thought she would die from the sheer happiness of the moment. *That damned agreement*. How often had she thought of it in just those words. "Yes," she whispered breathlessly.

"What else? That isn't enough, Leslie. This time, you have to let *me* give *you* something."

You have, my darling, she thought, *if only you knew how much*. But she knew he wouldn't believe her. She glanced down at his hand, resting on the slope of her breast and felt her flesh tingling beneath it, swelling, straining for his touch.

"There is one thing," she said softly, reaching to cover his hand with hers.

She heard his breath catch as she moved his hand ever so slightly lower.

"Something I missed," she said.

Now he needed no coaching. His hand cupped her breast, lifting it, kneading it gently.

"It might be difficult to arrange"—her voice broke from the exquisite pleasure his touch gave her, but she went on, almost without interruption—"with the crowd in the house."

"What is it, Leslie?" he murmured against her lips. "Anything."

"A—wedding night."

His eyes darkened, and his mouth slanted in a sensual promise. "That, my lovely, lovely lady, is exactly what I had in mind."

SECOND CHANCE AT LOVE

COMING NEXT MONTH

CONSPIRACY OF HEARTS #406 by Pat Dalton
Eric Trevor claims he's a spy protecting her
from danger, but Lisa Rollins is captivated by her
mysterious guardian—and that's where the danger lies...

HEAT WAVE #407 by Lee Williams
To Hollywood movie scout Nadine McGuane,
sleeping in the eye of a South American hurricane
seems simple—compared to tangling with
dashing anthropologist Zachary Matthews.

TEMPORARY ANGEL #408 by Courtney Ryan
Stung by hometown gossip and disapproval, Ashley Evans
turns to her platonic male roommate,
sexy musician Jesse Stark, for comfort...but
discovers unspoken passion instead...

HERO AT LARGE #409 by Steffie Hall
When unemployed carpenter Ken Callahan moves in
to perform "house husband" chores for skating coach
Chris Nelson, her heart's in more trouble than his career!

CHASING RAINBOWS #410 by Carole Buck
Paralegal Laura Newton's drawn to debonair, crusading
lawyer Kenyon C. Sutton—but his noble causes soon
bring him to battle with her prestigious Boston firm...

PRIMITIVE GLORY #411 by Cass McAndrew
Amanda Lacey finds that getting field agronomist
Eric Nichols to follow office procedures in the exotic
Himalayas is as impossible as resisting his heated embraces.

SECOND CHANCE AT LOVE

Be Sure to Read These New Releases!

NO HOLDS BARRED #394 by Jackie Leigh
Eli Sutherland's content being an investment
manager by day and wrestler Stud Savage by night...
until Kate Harcourt begins playing Stud's "girlfriend" and
turns his carefully planned life topsy-turvy.

DEVIN'S PROMISE #395 by Kelly Adams
Twelve years after their shared youth, the roguish,
irrepressible Devin O'Neill is back for good—
and Cass Heath's determined not to lose her heart
again to this Irish charmer...

FOR LOVE OF CHRISTY #396 by Jasmine Craig
When policewoman Laura Forbes marries America's
sexiest heartthrob, TV superstar Bennett Logan, to help
him win custody of his daughter Christy, their
marriage of convenience proves to be anything but!

WHISTLING DIXIE #397 by Adrienne Edwards
Engaged in an amorous battle, snake curator
Roberta E. Lee's determined not to surrender—but
Yankee banker Stephen Grant's planning
strategies guaranteed to besiege her southern heart.

BEST INTENTIONS #398 by Sherryl Woods
Tough-talking Traci Marie's got things under control—
until her freewheeling ex-husband Doug Maguire comes back
to see his son, charming his way into her heart...

NIGHT MOVES #399 by Jean Kent
When Drug Enforcement Administration officer Greg
Heflin investigates Kelsey Sviderskas, he finds himself
falling for this trusting Swedish beauty—
or is he falling for a clever innocence act?

Order on opposite page

SECOND CHANCE AT LOVE

Available at your local bookstore or return this form to:

SECOND CHANCE AT LOVE
THE BERKLEY PUBLISHING GROUP, Dept. B
390 Murray Hill Parkway, East Rutherford, NJ 07073

Please send me the titles checked above. I enclose _____ Include $1.00 for postage and handling if one book is ordered; add 25¢ per book for two or more not to exceed $1.75. CA, IL, NJ, NY, PA, and TN residents please add sales tax. Prices subject to change without notice and may be higher in Canada.

NAME_____

ADDRESS_____

CITY_____STATE/ZIP_____

(Allow six weeks for delivery.)   **SK-41b**

Highly Acclaimed
Historical Romances From Berkley